IMAGININGS

IMAGININGS

An Anthology of Visionary Literature

VOLUME ONE

AFTER THE MYTHS WENT HOME

Edited by **Stefan Rudnicki**

Introduction by Harlan Ellison

Frog, Ltd.
Berkeley, California

Published by Frog, Ltd.

Frog, Ltd. books are distributed by
North Atlantic Books
P.O. Box 12327
Berkeley, California 94712

Cover design by Brad Greene
Book design by Brad Greene
Printed in Canada

North Atlantic Books' publications are available through most bookstores. For further information, call 800-337-2665 or visit our website at www.northatlanticbooks.com.

Substantial discounts on bulk quantities are available to corporations, professional associations, and other organizations. For details and discount information, contact our special sales department.

Library of Congress Cataloging-in-Publication Data

Imaginings : an anthology of visionary literature / edited by Stefan Rudnicki ; introduction by Harlan Ellison.
    p. cm.
    ISBN 1-58394-094-4 (pbk.)
    1. Science fiction. 2. Fantasy fiction. 3. Mythology--Fiction. I. Rudnicki, Stefan, 1945-
    PN6120.95.S33I43 2004
    808.83'876—dc22

                                                              2003023030
                                                              CIP

1 2 3 4 5 6 7 8 9 TRANS 09 08 07 06 05 04

Special thanks to the living authors who lent *Imaginings* the light of their visions: John Crowley, Lewis Shiner, Robert Silverberg (who also contributed the volume's title), and the irrepressible Harlan Ellison. And thanks too to John Hunt, who encouraged and nurtured this project in its early stages; to Deborah DeCuir, whose fantasy art research, although unused, helped shape it, and to Richard Grossinger and Emma Moore who took it to its final form.

CONTENTS

Part Two

OTHER MYTHS

Introduction

LOFTY AMBITIONS

by Harlan Ellison

This is a *soigné* chrestomathy.

For those who speak even less idiomatic French than I, permit me to translate. *Soigné* is one of those words that mean more than its translation explicates. As with Latin and Yiddish and a few other deep and rich languages, it contains in its linguistic parameters an infinitude of shadings and interpretations. (*Ignorantia legis neminem excusat* and *l'esprit d'escalier* are two perfect examples.)

Soigné is best translated as meaning "carefully, or elegantly, done or designed; well-groomed."

Chrestomathy is merely a high-falutin' synonym for compendium, collection, anthology, ana, agglomeration, aggregate, mass, pile, mish-mosh, heap. But why such fastidious words?

When I am thrust in the company of the great, or the near-great—not just the faddish or controversial or infamous, the tabloid platypus-of-the-week, but the genuinely awe-inspiring—I am beset by an idiotic reaction-formation that thereafter makes me want to hide myself from sight by screwing myself into the ground and descending to a subterranean place where consummate darkness will shroud me from the ridicule of my betters. And casual onlookers. What happens is this:

I feel the bumpkin. Just fell off the turnip truck. Spots on my tie, shoes unshined, baggy in the seat of my pants, a clod, a yokel, a kadodie from the sticks. My tongue, sadly, does not get tangled over my eye-teeth so I cannot see what I am saying; it just begins to flop, to blabber and gibber and go on in an obstinately endless farrago of dumbass remarks. And all of them in velvet verbiage. Purple into the ultraviolet. Words whose meanings I've forgotten, or never knew; sentences so prolix that little girls in Harlem could use them for their Double-Dutch exercises; imprecisions and redundancies that make hip-hop and rap lyrics seem like the most golden moments of Langston Hughes. In short, I demonstrate a feeling of inferiority and stunned idolatry that clearly screams, "mayday! mayday!"

As with one of the dippy characters played by Mike Myers and Dana Carvey in the "Wayne's World" skits, on very rare occasions a clarity of perception comes to me when I am out of my depth, playing in a game too rich for my blood, way in over my head, and I fall to my knees, wrench at my forelock, and genuflect as I cry, "I'm unworthy! Unworthy, I say: unworthy!"

Brought to this place to bid you welcome, I stand wholly unadorned and ignoble, sweating like a barnyard animal, abruptly confronted with the realization that my credentials aren't worth a buttonhook when it comes to prefacing this collection properly. It is a *soigné* chrestomathy. And I am a ragamuffin.

Hark. Note these sage observations from more than fifty years of reading and editing anthologies:

The halcyon days of brilliant anthologists are long gone, my friends. The salvo of names I now fire at you will either patter meaninglessly on the tin roof of your ignorance, or blast through the walls of memory to light up your eyes with glorious recollections. Groff Conklin. Bennett Cerf. Phil Stong. The cousins Fred Dannay and Manfred B. Lee who wrote and edited as "Ellery Queen." Frederik Pohl. August Derleth. Christine Campbell Thompson. If you are the former, with a tin roof and tin ear, those named will be merely white noise. But trust me, young sirs and mesdames, giants walked on Earth in those days. Those suckers knew how to put together bookoo def chrestomathies. But Augie is dead, and so is Groff Conklin, and with very few exceptions these days what passes for an anthology is no better—and often much worse—than an average issue of a digest-sized monthly magazine.

What happened was that the market changed. And what Fred Pohl had done with the *Star Science Fiction* anthologies for Ballantine in the '50s—extraordinary books with superlative and even experimental stories—what I had done with the two *Dangerous Visions* anthologies in the late '60s and early '70s—became the model for the most marketable anthologies: original fiction, written to order.

So instead of culling the best (or even most overlooked) stories of generations, writers of minimal talent were engaged to write fiction to a narrow theme:

SHORT STUFFS: Stories of people under four foot three.

PLAGUE BEARERS: Stories about acne, wens, running sores, and alien pustulants.

FUTURE HUSBANDRY: Stories of sex with animatronic animals.

WHINING WOMEN: Stories of Those Who Need to Discover Their True Identities.

SYKOTIC SWORDSMEN: Stories of meanness, madness, masculine road rage, and brawny brutality.

Well, yes, those are feverish conjurations of my own snappish personality, but the real jokes were equally as dumb and disposable. Yet, as I say, the market changed, and no longer was there a place for the carefully crafted collections of elegant and intelligently themed stories. The audience—so said the johnny and jenny-come-latelies who swarmed the Manhattan bailiwicks—had read Bradbury's "Mars Is Heaven" one time too many. Nobody gave a damn any more about Henry Kuttner and C.L. Moore's "Vintage Season." The constituency for appreciating Jim Blish's "Surface Tension" was too old and arteriosclerotic to pay any attention, and besides, they already had the story in a Damon Knight anthology published forty years ago.

The worshipful twits whom Dickens had in mind when he wrote, "Any book you have not read is a *new* book," brought their focus-group fancies to the bookstalls, and they truly convinced themselves that a collection of twelve specially commissioned stories by some good, some mediocre, some hack, some just plain awful writers could compare to an anthology carefully selected from all the best work available since the story of Gilgamesh.

Well, that's where we find ourselves today. And the anthology is practically a dodo. There are still paperback originals being cranked out with themes as thin as Jennifer Aniston's shadow, and they sell miserably, and writers waste their time pounding that sand into the carcasses, only to see their work vanish overnight.

The great old idea of editing an anthology that would stand the test of time, be readable and worth remembering fifty years after publication, well, that's an ideal fit only for geezers.

What the world needs now ain't love sweet love, it's a *soigné* chrestomathy. Something that can hold its head high and look to the stars. A book with lofty ambitions.

But where do we find an anthologist who has the mettle, the intellect, the wide-ranging intellectual fecundity, the diversity, the *balls* (or eggs) to do the job?

Don't look at me, bro. I've still got *The Last Dangerous Visions* to complete. But here I am to introduce, to greet, to herald the Charles Foster Kane to your tin roof, tin ear— Tiny Tim Cratchit.

Stefan Rudnicki. Say it with me: Stefan Rudnicki. Steff *On.* Rudd *Nick* Eeee.

Speaks fluent French, Swedish, Polish, German, and English. And stumbles more eloquently around half a dozen others than you or I with our native tongue. Columbia-educated in the Liberal Arts, with an English degree, he has lived in Stockholm and Montreal and New York and Kraków. He is very likely the finest director of spoken word audio in America today. The list of Grammy, Audie, Listen Up, Bram Stoker, and Ray Bradbury awards and nominations runs to several pages. He has directed more than four hundred spoken word albums with hundreds and hundreds of celebrity readers. He is currently the Creative Director of Fantastic Audio. And on, and on, *pace, pace!*

He is the Great Designer behind this rare and precious anthology, this *soigné* chrestomathy of fantastic dreams and lofty ambitions.

Check the table of contents. This is not another of those bloodshot, spavined, swaybacked old dray-mules sand-stuffed with the nine millionth reprint of "Star Slaves of the Inner Ear" or some freshly PC'd bit of hackwork by a writer with three names of whom you've never heard previously.

Oliver Onions is cheek-by-jowl with Anne McCaffrey. Fritz Leiber and John Shirley sail beside Jonathan Swift and Nikolai Gogol. Poe and LeGuin and Asimov pull the oars next to Clark Ashton Smith and Homer and Dante. Oh, my friends, this … *this* is a book with lofty, I say *lofty* ambitions! Can I have an "Amen"? Thank yuh!

This is a book that says the literature of imagination is the oldest, most enriching form of storytelling our mere species has ever conceived. It is eternal. It stretches back to the writings of Solon and Strabo and Aristophanes, and comes to us anew each decade in novels of the fantastic, in pulp magazines, in Big Little Books and comics, and the writing of Barthelme and Oates and Chabon. It is the wellspring of ideas that sooner or later sweeten the elixir of mainstream writing.

But without books like this, without anthologies that have lofty ambitions, the well stinks of moss and mold and self-indulgence. I present to you Mr. Rudnicki, and his marvelous animatronic *soigné* chrestomathy. Enjoy.

Part One

THE MYTHS WE LIVE BY

"A YOUTH IN APPAREL THAT GLITTERED …"

Stephen Crane

From *The Black Riders*, 1895

A youth in apparel that glittered
Went to walk in a grim forest.
There he met an assassin
Attired all in garb of old days;
He, scowling through the thickets,
And dagger poised quivering,
Rushed upon the youth.
"Sir," said the latter.
"I am enchanted, believe me,
To die, thus,
In this medieval fashion,
According to the legends;
Ah, what joy!"
Then took he the wound, smiling,
And died, content.

In Hamlet's words, "There is nothing either good or bad, but thinking makes it so...." We are the sources of our deepest fears and highest aspirations.

But the thinking of things, the imagining of them, requires a vocabulary. Vocabulary is not just words, of course, but images, associations, and constructs as well. And words themselves are meaningful only insofar as they resonate with our dreams and sensations. We make up stories to justify and give meaning to our lives, our time, our humanity. These stories are the myths we live by, whether we are aware of them or not. We seem to need to populate our world with contexts. After all, what action can be considered correct, or even important, without a context? And these contexts, too, are the myths.

AFTER THE MYTHS
WENT HOME

Robert Silverberg

First published in Fantasy and *Science Fiction*, 1969

"After the Myths Went Home" suggests, in a science fiction mode, what might happen if we were to try to live without myths. Quite simply, and with some terror, Silverberg concludes, "And we are alone." Robert Silverberg's career has been marked by a particular preponderance and awareness of myths as the grounding sources of action and imagination, so it is no wonder that he selected this story as one of his favorites.

For a while in those years we were calling great ones out of the past, to find out what they were like. This was in the middle twelves—12400 to 12450, say. We called up Caesar and Anthony, and also Cleopatra. We got Freud and Marx and Lenin into the same room and let them talk. We summoned Winston Churchill, who was a disappointment (he lisped and drank too much), and Napoleon, who was magnificent. We raided ten millennia of history for our sport.

But after half a century of this we grew bored with our game. We were easily bored, in the middle twelves. So we started to call up the myth people, the gods and the heroes.

That seemed more romantic, and this was one of Earth's romanticist eras we lived in.

It was my turn then to serve as curator of the Hall of Man, and that was where they built the machine, so I watched it going up from the start. Leor the Builder was in charge. He had made the machines that called the real people up, so this was only slightly different, no real challenge to his talents. He had to feed in another kind of data, full of archetypes and psychic currents, but the essential process of reconstruction would be the same. He never had any doubt of success.

Leor's new machine had crystal rods and silver sides. A giant emerald was embedded in its twelve-sided lid. Tinsel streamers of radiant platinum dangled from the ebony struts on which it rose.

"Mere decoration," Leor confided to me. "I could have made a simple black box. But brutalism is out of fashion."

The machine sprawled all over the Pavilion of Hope on the north face of the Hall of Man. It hid the lovely flicker-mosaic flooring, but at least it cast lovely reflections into the mirrored surfaces of the exhibit cases. Somewhere about 12570, Leor said he was ready to put his machine into operation.

We arranged the best possible weather. We tuned the winds, deflecting the westerlies a bit and pushing all clouds far to the south. We sent up new moons to dance at night in wondrous patterns, now and again coming together to spell out Leor's name. People came from all over Earth, thousands of them, camping in whisper-tents on the great plain that begins at the Hall of Man's doorstep. There was real excitement then, a tension that crackled beautifully through the clear blue air.

Leor made his last adjustments. The committee of literary advisers conferred with him over the order of events, and there was some friendly bickering. We chose daytime for the first demonstration, and tinted the sky light purple for better effect. Most of us put on our youngest bodies, though there were some who said they wanted to look mature in the presence of these fabled figures out of time's dawn.

"Whenever you wish to begin—" Leor said.

There were speeches first. Chairman Peng gave his usual lighthearted address. The Procurator of Pluto, who was visiting us, congratulated Leor on the fertility of his inventions. Nistim, then in his third or fourth successive term as Metabolizer General, encouraged everyone present to climb to a higher level. Then the master of ceremonies pointed to me. No, I said, shaking my head, I am a very poor speaker. They replied that it was my duty, as curator of the Hall of Man, to explain what was about to unfold.

Reluctantly, I came forward.

"You will see the dreams of old mankind made real today," I said, groping for words. "The hopes of the past will walk among you, and so, I think, will the nightmares. We are offering you a view of the imaginary figures by means of whom the ancients attempted to give structure to the universe. These gods, these heroes summed up patterns of cause and effect, and served as organizing forces around which cultures could crystallize. It is all very strange to us and it will be wonderfully interesting. Thank you."

Leor was given the signal to begin.

"I must explain one thing," he said. "Some of the beings you are about to see were purely imaginary, concocted by tribal poets, even as my friend has just told you. Others, though, were based on actual human beings who once

7

walked the Earth as ordinary mortals, and who were trans-figured, given more-than-human qualities, raised to the pantheon. Until they actually appear, we will not know which figures belong to which category, but I can tell you how to detect their origin once you see them. Those who were human beings before they became myths will have a slight aura, a shadow, a darkness in the air about them. This is the lingering trace of their essential humanity, which no myth-maker can erase. So I learned in my preliminary experiments. I am now ready."

Leor disappeared into the bowels of his machine. A single pure note, high and clean, rang in the air. Suddenly, on the stage looking out to the plain, there emerged a naked man, blinking, peering around.

Leor's voice, from within the machine, said, "This is Adam, the first of all men."

And so the gods and the heroes came back to us on that brilliant afternoon in the middle twelves, while all the world watched in joy and fascination.

Adam walked across the stage and spoke to Chairman Peng, who solemnly saluted him and explained what was taking place. Adam's hand was outspread over his loins. "Why am I naked?" Adam asked. "It is wrong to be naked."

I pointed out to him that he had been naked when he first came into the world, and that we were merely showing respect for authenticity by summoning him back that way.

"But I have eaten the apple," Adam said. "Why do you bring me back conscious of shame, and give me nothing to conceal my shame? Is this proper? Is this consistent? If you want a naked Adam, bring forth an Adam who has not yet eaten the apple. But—"

Leor's voice broke in: "This is Eve, the mother of us all."

Eve stepped forth, naked also, though her long silken hair hid the curve of her breasts. Unashamed, she smiled and held out her hand to Adam, who rushed to her, crying, "Cover yourself! Cover yourself!"

Surveying the thousands of onlookers, Eve said coolly, "Why should I, Adam? These people are naked too, and this must be Eden again."

"This is not Eden," said Adam. "This is the world of our children's children's children's children."

"I like this world," Eve said. "Relax."

Leor announced the arrival of Pan the Goat-Footed.

Now Adam and Eve both were surrounded by the dark aura of essential humanity. I was surprised at this, since I doubted that there had ever been a First Man and a First Woman on whom legends could be based; yet I assumed that this must be some symbolic representation of the concept of man's evolution. But Pan the half-human monster also wore the aura. Had there been such a being in the real world?

I did not understand it then. But later I came to see that if there had never been a goat-footed man, there nevertheless had been men who behaved as Pan behaved, and out of them that lusty god had been created. As for the Pan who came out of Leor's machine, he did not remain long on the stage. He plunged forward into the audience, laughing and waving his arms and kicking his cloven hooves in the air. "Great Pan lives!" He seized in his arms the slender form of Milian, the year-wife of Divud the Archivist, and carried her away toward a grove of feather-trees on the horizon.

"He does me honor," said Milian's year-husband Divud.

Leor continued to toil in his machine.

He brought forth Hector and Achilles, Orpheus, Perseus, Loki, and Absalom. He brought forth Medea, Cassandra,

Odysseus, Oedipus. He brought forth Thoth, the Minotaur, Aeneas, Salome. He brought forth Shiva and Gilgamesh, Viracocha and Pandora, Priapus and Astarte, Diana, Diomedes, Dionysus, Deucalion. The afternoon waned and the sparkling moons sailed into the sky, and still Leor labored. He gave us Clytemnestra and Agamemnon, Helen and Menelaus, Isis and Osiris. He gave us Damballa and Guedenibo and Papa Legba. He gave us Baal. He gave us Samson. He gave us Krishna. He woke Quetzalcoatl, Adonis, Holger Dansk, Kali, Ptah, Thor, Jason, Nimrod, Set.

The darkness deepened and the creatures of myth jostled and tumbled on the stage, and overflowed onto the plain. They mingled with one another, old enemies exchanging gossip, old friends clasping hands, members of the same pantheon embracing or looking warily upon their rivals. They mixed with us, too, the heroes selecting women, the monsters trying to seem less monstrous, the gods shopping for worshippers.

Perhaps we had enough. But Leor would not stop. This was his time of glory.

Out of the machine came Roland and Oliver, Rustum and Sohrab, Cain and Abel, Damon and Pythias, Orestes and Pylades, Jonathan and David. Out of the machine came St. George, St. Vitus, St. Nicholas, St. Christopher, St. Valentine, St. Jude. Out of the machine came the Furies, the Harpies, the Pleiades, the Fates, the Norms. Leor was a romantic, and he knew no moderation.

All who came forth wore the aura of humanity.

But wonders pall. The Earthfolk of the middle twelves were easily distracted and easily bored. The cornucopia of miracles was far from exhausted, but on the fringes of the audience I saw people talking to the sky and heading for home. We who were close to Leor had to remain, of course, though we were surfeited by these fantasies and baffled by their abundance.

An old white-bearded man wrapped in a heavy aura left the machine. He carried a slender metal tube. "This is Galileo," said Leor.

"Who is he?" the Procurator of Pluto asked me, for Leor, growing weary, had ceased to describe his conjured ghosts.

I had to request the information from an output in the Hall of Man. "A latter-day god of science," I told the Procurator, "who is credited with discovering the stars. Believed to have been a historical personage before his deification, which occurred after his martyrdom by religious conservatives."

Now that the mood was on him, Leor summoned more of these gods of science, Newton and Einstein and Hippocrates and Copernicus and Oppenheimer and Freud. We had met some of them before, in the days when we were bringing real people out of lost time, but now they had new guises, for they had passed through the mythmakers' hands. They bore emblems of their special functions, symbols of knowledge and power, and they went among us offering to heal, to teach, to explain. They were nothing like the real Newton and Einstein and Freud we had seen. They stood three times the height of men, and lightning played around their brows.

Then came a tall, bearded man with a bloodied head. "Abraham Lincoln," said Leor.

"The ancient god of emancipation," I told the Procurator, after some research.

Then came a handsome young man with a dazzling smile and also a bloodied head. "John Kennedy," said Leor.

"The ancient god of youth and springtime," I told the Procurator. "A symbol of the change of seasons, of the defeat of summer by winter."

"That was Osiris," said the Procurator. "Why are there two?"

"There are many more," I said. "Baldur, Tammuz, Mithra, Attis."

"Why did they need so many?" he asked.

Leor said, "Now I will stop."

The gods and heroes were among us. A season of revelry began.

Medea went off with Jason, and Agamemnon was reconciled with Clytemnestra, and Theseus and the Minotaur took up lodgings together. Others preferred the company of men. I spoke a while with John Kennedy, the last of the myths to come from the machine. Like Adam, the first, he was troubled at being here.

"I was no myth," he insisted. "I lived. I was real. I entered primaries and made speeches."

"You became a myth," I said. "You lived and died and in your dying you were transfigured."

He chuckled. "Into Osiris? Into Baldur?"

"It seems appropriate."

"To you, maybe. They stopped believing in Baldur a thousand years before I was born."

"To me," I said, "you and Osiris and Baldur are contemporaries. To me and all the people here. You are of the ancient world. You are thousands of years removed from us."

"And I'm the last myth you let out of the machine?"

"You are."

"Why? Did men stop making myths after the twentieth century?"

"You would have to ask Leor. But I think you are right: your time was the end of the age of myth-making. After your time we could no longer believe such things as myths. We did not *need* myths. When we passed out of the era of troubles we entered a kind of paradise where every one of us lived a myth of his own, and then why should we have to raise some men to great heights among us?"

He looked at me strangely. "Do you really believe that? That you live in paradise? That men have become gods?"

"Spend some time in our world," I said, "and see for yourself."

He went out into the world, but what his conclusions were I never knew, for I did not speak to him again. Often I encountered roving gods and heroes, though. They were everywhere. They quarreled and looted and ran amok, some of them, but we were not very upset by that, since it was how we expected archetypes out of the dawn to act. And some were gentle. I had a brief love affair with Persephone. I listened, enchanted, to the singing of Orpheus. Krishna danced for me.

Dionysus revived the lost art of making liquors, and taught us to drink and be drunk.

Loki made magics of flame for us.

Taliesin crooned incomprehensible, wondrous ballads to us.

Achilles hurled his javelin for us.

It was a season of wonder, but the wonder ebbed. The mythfolk began to bore us. There were too many of them, and they were too loud, too active, too demanding. They wanted us to love them, listen to them, bow to them, write poems about them. They asked questions—some of them, anyway—that pried into the inner workings of our world, and embarrassed us, for we scarcely knew the answers. They grew vicious and schemed against each other, sometimes causing perils for us.

Leor had provided us with a splendid diversion. But we all agreed it was time for the myths to go home. We had had them with us for fifty years, and that was quite enough.

We rounded them up, and started to put them back into the machine.

The heroes were the easiest to catch, for all their strength. We hired Loki to trick them into returning to the Hall of Man. "Mighty tasks await you there," he told them, and they hurried thence to show their valor. Loki led them into the machine and scurried out, and Leor sent them away, Herakles, Achilles, Hector, Perseus, Cuchulainn, and the rest of the energetic breed.

After that many of the demonic ones came. They said they were bored with us as we were with them and went back into the machine of their free will. Thus departed Kali, Legba, Set, and many more.

Some we had to trap and take by force. Odysseus disguised himself as Breel, the secretary to Chairman Pang, and would have fooled us forever if the real Breel, returning from holiday in Jupiter, had not exposed the hoax. And then Odysseus struggled. Loki gave us problems. Oedipus launched blazing curses when we came for him. Daedalus clung touchingly to Leor and begged, "Let me stay, brother! Let me stay!" and had to be thrust within.

Year after year the task of finding and capturing them continued, and one day we knew we had them all. The last to go was Cassandra, who had been living alone in a distant island, clad in rags.

"Why did you send for us?" she asked. "And, having sent, why do you ship us away?"

"The game is over," I said to her. "We will turn now to other sports."

"You should have kept us," Cassandra said. "People who have no myths of their own would do well to borrow those of others, and not just as sport. Who will comfort your souls in the dark times ahead? Who will guide your spirits when the suffering begins? Who will explain the woe that will befall you? Woe! Woe!"

"The woes of Earth," I said gently, "lie in Earth's past. We need no myths."

Cassandra smiled and stepped into the machine. And was gone.

And then the age of fire and turmoil opened, for when the myths went home the invaders came, bursting from the sky. And our towers toppled and our moons fell. And the cold-eyed strangers went among us, doing as they wished with us.

And those of us who survived cried out to the old gods, the vanished heroes.

"Loki, come!"

"Achilles, defend us!"

"Shiva, release us!"

"Herakles! Thor! Gawain!"

But the gods are silent, and the heroes do not come. The machine that glittered in the Hall of Man is broken. Leor, its maker, is gone from this world. Jackals run through our gardens, and our masters stride in our streets, and we are made slaves. And we are alone beneath the frightful sky. And we are alone.

NOVELTY

John Crowley

From *Novelty: Four Stories*, 1989

John Crowley has been a master at creating complex worlds that often coexist with ours, sometimes intersecting in wonderful and dangerous ways. In "Novelty," he gives us a glimpse into the act of creation itself. Mixing religion with psychology and literary inspiration, he allows us into the interior of the process, giving us a kind of story *about* the imagination. Is this science fiction? Definitely not. Fantasy? Probably not. Reality? Yes, the private reality of the creative mind ... imagination.

I

He found, quite suddenly and just as he took a stool midway down the bar, that he had been vouchsafed a theme. A notion about the nature of things that he had been turning over in his mind for some time had become, without his ever choosing it, the theme of a book. It had "fallen into place" as it's put, like the tumblers of a lock that a safecracker listens to, and—so he experienced it—with the same small, smooth sound.

The theme was the contrary pull men feel between Novelty and Security. Between boredom and adventure, between safety and dislocation, between the snug and the wild. Yes! Not only a grand human theme, but a truly *mammalian* theme, perhaps the only one. Curiosity killed the cat, we are warned, and warned with good reason, and yet we are curious. Cats could be a motif: cats asleep, taking their ease in that superlatively comfortable way they have—you feel drowsy and snug just watching them. Cats on the prowl, endlessly prying. Cats tiptoe-walking away from fearsome novelty, hair on fire and faces shocked. He chuckled, pleased with this, and lifted the glass that had been set before him. From the great window south light poured through the golden liquor, refracted delicately by ice.

The whole front of the Seventh Saint Bar & Grill where he sat is of glass, floor to ceiling, a glass divided by vertical beams into a triptych and deeply tinted brown. During the day nothing of the dimly lit interior of the bar can be seen from the outside; walkers-by see only themselves, darkly; often they stop to adjust their clothing or their hair in what seems to them to be a mirror, or simply gaze at themselves in passing, momentarily but utterly absorbed, unaware that they are caught at it by watchers inside. (Or watcher, today, he being so far the bar's sole customer.) Seen from inside the bar, the avenue, the stores opposite, the street glimpsed going off at right angles, the trapezoid of sky visible above the lower buildings, are altered by the tinted windows into an elsewhere, oddly peaceful, a desert or the interior of the sea. Sometimes when he has fallen asleep face upward in the sun, his dreams have taken on this quality of supernatural bright darkness.

Novelty. Security. *Novelty* wouldn't be a bad title. It had the grandness of abstraction, alerting the reader that large and thoughtful things were to be bodied forth. As yet he had no inkling of any incidents or characters that might occupy his theme; perhaps he never would. He could see through the book itself, he could feel its closed heft and see it opened, white pages comfortably large and shadowed gray by print; dense, numbered, full of meat. He sensed the narrative voice, speaking calmly and precisely, with immense assurance building, building; a voice too far off for him to hear, but speaking.

The door of the bar opened, showing him a momentary oblong of true daylight, blankly white. A woman entered. He couldn't see her face as she crossed to the bar in front of the window, but he could see, drawn with exactitude by the light behind her, her legs within a summery white dress. When young he had supposed, without giving it much thought, that women didn't realize that sun behind them revealed them in this way; now he supposes that of course they must, and thinks about it.

"Well, look who's here," said the bartender. "You off today?"

"I took off," she said, and as she took a seat between him and the window, he saw that she was known to him, that is, they had sat here in this relation before. "I couldn't stand it anymore. What's tall and cool and not too alcoholic?"

"How about a spritzer?"

"Okay."

He caught himself staring fixedly at her, trying to remember if they had spoken before, and she caught him, too, raising her eyes to him as she lifted the pale drink to her lips, large dark eyes with startling whites; and looked away again quickly.

Where was he again? Novelty, security. He felt the feet of his attention skate out from under him in opposite directions. Should he make a note? He felt for the smooth shape of his pen in his pocket. "Theme for a novel: The contrary pull...." No. If this notion were real, he needn't make a note. A notion on which a note had to be made would be stillborn anyway; his notebook was a parish register of such, born and dead on the same page. Let it live if it can.

But had he spoken to her before? What had he said?

II

When he was in college, a famous poet made a useful distinction for him. He had drunk enough in the poet's company to be compelled to describe to him a poem he was thinking of. It would be a monologue of sorts, the self-contemplation of a student on a summer afternoon who is reading *Euphues.* The poem itself would be a subtle series of euphemisms, translating the heat, the day, the student's concerns, into symmetrical posies; translating even his contempt and boredom with that famously foolish book into a euphemism.

The poet nodded his big head in a sympathetic, rhythmic way as this was explained to him, then told him that there are two kinds of poems. There is the kind you write; there is the kind you talk about in bars. Both kinds have value and both are poems; but it's fatal to confuse them.

In the Seventh Saint, many years later, it has struck him that the difference between himself and Shakespeare wasn't talent—not especially—but *nerve.* The capacity not to be frightened by his largest and most potent conceptions, to simply (simply!) sit down and execute them. The dreadful lassitude he felt when something really large and multifarious came suddenly clear to him, something *Lear*-sized yet sonnet-precise. If only they didn't rush on him whole, all at once, massive and perfect, leaving him frightened and nerveless at the prospect of articulating them word by scene by page. He would try to believe they were of the kind told in bars, not the kind to be written, though there was no way to be sure of this except to attempt the writing; he would raise a finger (the novelist in the bar mirror raising the obverse finger) and push forward his change. Wailing like a neglected ghost, the vast notion would beat its wings into the void.

Sometimes it would pursue him for days and years as he fled desperately. Sometimes he would turn to face it, and do battle. Once, twice, he had been victorious, objectively at least. Out of an immense concatenation of feeling, thought, word, and transcendent meaning had come for his first novel, a slim, silent pageant of a book, tombstone for his slain conception. A publisher had taken it, gingerly; had slipped it quietly into the deep pool of spring releases, where it sank without a ripple, and where he supposes it lies still, its calm Bodoni gone long since green. A second, just as slim but more lurid, nightmarish even, about imaginary murders in an imaginary exotic locale, had been sold for a movie, though the movie had never been made. He felt guilt for the producer's failure (which perhaps the producer didn't feel), having known the book could not be filmed; he had made a large sum, enough to finance years of this kind of thing, on a book whose first printing was largely returned.

His editor now and then took him to an encouraging lunch, and talked about royalties, advances, and upcoming titles, letting him know that whatever doubts he had she considered him a member of the profession, and deserving of a share in its largesse and its gossip; at their last one, some months before, she had pressed him for a new book, something more easily graspable than his others. "A couple of chapters, and an outline," she said. "I could tell from that."

Well, he *was* sort of thinking of something, but it wasn't really shaping up, or rather it was shaping up rather like the others, into something indescribable at bottom.... "What it would be," he said timidly, "would be sort of a Catholic novel, about growing up Catholic," and she looked warily up at him over her Campari.

The first inkling of this notion had come to him the Christmas before, at his daughter's place in Vermont. On Christmas Eve, as indifferent evening took hold in the blue squares of the windows, he sat alone in the crepuscular kitchen, imbued with a profound sense of the identity of winter and twilight, of twilight and time, of time and memory, of his childhood and that Church which on this night waited to celebrate the second greatest of its feasts. For a moment or an hour as he sat, become one with the blue of the snow and silence, a congruity of star, cradle, winter, sacrament, self, it was as though he listened to a voice that had long been trying to catch his attention, to tell him, Yes, this was the subject long withheld from him, which he now knew, and must eventually act on.

He had managed, though, to avoid it. He only brought it out now to please his editor, at the same time aware that it wasn't what she had in mind at all. But he couldn't do better; he had really only the one subject, if subject was the word for it, this idea of a notion or a holy thing growing clear in the stream of time, being made manifest in unexpected ways to an assortment of people: the revelation itself wasn't important, it could be anything, almost. Beyond that he had only one interest, the seasons, which he could describe endlessly and with all the passion of a country-bred boy grown old in the city. He was coming to doubt (he said) that he wasn't a novelist at all, but a failed poet, like a failed priest, one who had perceived that in fact he had no vocation, had renounced his vows, and yet had found nothing at all else in the world worth doing when measured by the calling he didn't have, and went on through life fatally attracted to whatever of the sacerdotal he could find or invent in whatever occupation he fell into, plumbing or psychiatry or tending bar.

III

"Boring, boring, *boring*," said the woman down the bar from him. "I feel like taking off for good." Victor, the bartender, chin in his hand and elbow on the bar, looked at her with the remote sympathy of confessors and bartenders.

"Just take off," she said.

"So take off," Victor said. "Jeez, there's a whole world out there."

She made a small noise to indicate she doubted there was. Her brilliant eyes, roving over her prospects, fell on his where they were reflected in the bar mirror. She gazed at him but (he knew) didn't see him, for she was looking within. When she did focus and understand she was being regarded, she smiled briefly and glanced at his real person, then bent to her drink again. He summoned the bartender.

"Another, please, Victor."

"How's the writing coming?"

"Slowly. Very slowly. I just now thought of a new one, though."

"Izzat so."

It was so; but even as he said it, as the stirring-stick he had just raised out of the glass dripped whiskey drop by drop back into it, the older notion, the notion he had been unable at all adequately to describe to his editor, which he had long since dropped or thought he had dropped, stirred within him. Stirred mightily, though he tried to shut doors on it; stirred, rising, and came forth suddenly in all the panoply with which he had forgotten it had had come to be dressed, its facets glittering, windows opening on vistas, great draperies billowing. It seemed to have grown old in its seclusion but more potent, and fiercely reproachful of his neglect. Alarmed, he tried to shelter his tender new notion of Novelty and Security from its onrush, but even as he attempted this, the old notion seized upon the new, and he watched helplessly, the two couple in an utter ravishment and interlacement, made for each other, one thing now and more than twice as compelling as each had been before. "Jesus," he said aloud; and then looked up, wondering if he had been heard. Victor and the woman were tête-à-tête, talking urgently in undertones.

IV

"I know, I know," he said, raising a hand to forestall his editor's objection. "The Catholic Church is a joke. Especially the Catholic Church I grew up in ..."

"Sometimes a grim joke."

"And it's been told a lot. The nuns, the weird rules, all that decayed scholastic guff. The prescriptions, and the proscriptions—especially the proscriptions, all so trivial when they weren't hurtful or just ludicrous. But that's not the way it's perceived. For a kid, for me, the Church organized the whole world—not morally, either, or not especially, but in its whole nature. Even if the kid isn't particularly moved by thoughts of God and sin—I wasn't—there's still a lot of Church left over, do you see? Because all the important things about the Church were real things: objects, places, words, sights, smells, days. The liturgical calendar. The Eastern church must be even more so. For me, the Church was mostly about the seasons: it kept them in order. The Church was coextensive with the world."

"So the kid's point of view against—"

"No, no. What I would do, see, to get around this contradiction between the real Church and this other Church I seemed to experience physically and emotionally, is to reimagine the Catholic Church as another kind of church altogether, a very subtle and wise church, that understood all these feelings; a church that was really—secretly—*about* these things in fact, and not what it seemed to be about; and then pretend, in the book, that the church I grew up in was that church."

"You're going to invent a whole new religion?"

"Well, not exactly. It would just be a matter of shifting emphasis, somehow, turning a thing a hundred and eighty degrees ..."

"Well, how? Do you mean 'books in the running brooks, sermons in stones,' that kind of thing? Pantheism?"

"No. No. The opposite. In that kind of religion the trees and the sky and the weather *stand for* God or some kind of supernatural unity. In my religion, God and all the rituals and sacraments would stand for the real world. The religion would be a means of perceiving the real world in a sacramental way. A Gnostic ascension. A secret at the heart of it. And the secret is—everything. Common reality. The day outside the church window."

"Hm."

"That's what it would really have been about from the beginning. And only seemed to be about these divine personages, and stuff, and these rules."

She nodded slowly in a way that showed she followed him but frankly saw no novel. He went on, wanting as least to say it all before he no longer saw it with this clarity. "The priests and nuns would know this was the case, the wisest of them, and would guide the worshipers—the ones they thought could grasp it—to see through the paradox, to see that it *is* a paradox: that only by believing, wholly and deeply, in all of it could you see through one day to what is real—see through Christmas to the snow; see through the fasting, and the saints' lives, and the sins, and Baby Jesus walking through the snow every Christmas night ringing a little bell—"

"What?"

"That was a story one told. That was a thing she said was the case."

"Good heavens. Did she believe it?"

"Who knows? That's what I'm getting at."

She broke into her eggs Florentine with a delicate fork. The two chapters, full of meat; the spinach of an outline. She was very attractive in a coltish, aristocratic way, with a *framboise* flush on her tanned cheeks that was just the flush his wife's cheeks had had. No doubt still had; no doubt.

"Like Zen," he said desperately. "As though it were a kind of Zen."

V

Well, he had known as well as she that it was no novel, no matter that it importuned him, reminding him often of its deep truth to his experience, and suggesting shyly how much fun it might be to manipulate, what false histories he could invent that would account for the Church he imagined. But he had it now; now the world began to turn beneath him firmly, both rotating and revolving; it was quite clear now.

The *theme* would not be religion at all, but this ancient conflict between Novelty and Security. This theme would be embodied in the contrasted adventures of a set of *characters*, a family of Catholic believers modeled on his own. The *motion* of the book would be the sense of a holy thing ripening in the stream of time, that is, the seasons; and the *form* would be a false history or mirror-reversal of the world he had known and the Church he had believed in.

Absurdly, his heart had begun to beat fast. Not years from now, not months, very soon, imaginably soon, he could begin. That there was still nothing concrete in what he envisioned didn't bother him, for he was sure this scheme was one that would generate concreteness spontaneously and easily. He had planted a banner amid his memories and imaginings, a banner to which they could all repair, to which they were repairing even now, primitive clans vivified by these colors, clamoring to be marshaled into troops by the captains of his art.

It would take a paragraph, a page, to eliminate, say, the Reformation, and thus make his Church infinitely more aged, bloated, old in power, forgetful of dogmas long grown universal and ignorable, dogmas altered by subtle subversives into their opposites, by a brotherhood within the enormous bureaucracy of faith, a brotherhood animated by a holy irony and secret as the Rosicrucians. Or contrariwise: he could pretend that the Reformation had been more nearly a complete success than it was, leaving his Roman faith a small, inward-turning, Gnostic sect, poor and not grand, guiltless of the Inquisition; its Pope itinerant or in shabby exile somewhere (Douai, or Alexandria, or Albany); through Appalachia a poor priest travels from church to church, riding the circuit in an old Studebaker as rusty black as his cassock, putting up at a gaunt frame house on the outskirts of town, a convent. The wainscoted parlor is the nuns' chapel, and the pantry is full of their canning; in autumn the broken stalks of corn wither in their kitchen garden. "Use it up, wear it out," says the proverb of their creed (and not that of splendid and orgulous Protestants), "make it do, do without": and they possess themselves in edgeworn and threadbare Truth.

Yes! The little clapboard church in Kentucky where his family had worshipped, in the Depression, amid the bumptious Baptists. In the hastening dawn he had walked a mile to serve six o'clock mass there. In winter the stove's smell was incense; in summer it was the damp odor of morning coming through the lancet windows, opened a crack to reveal a band of blue-green day beneath the feet of the saints fragilely pictured there in imitation stained glass. The three or four old Polish women always present always took Communion, their extended tongues trembling and their veined closed eyelids trembling, too; and though when they rose crossing themselves they became only unsanctified old women again, he had for a moment glimpsed their clean souls. There were aged and untended rose bushes on the sloping lawn of the big gray house he had grown up in—his was by far the best off of any family in that little parish—

and when the roses bloomed in May the priest came and the familiar few they saw in church each week gathered, and the Virgin was crowned there, a Virgin pink and blue and white as the rose-burdened day, the best lace tablecloth beneath her, strange to see that domestic lace outdoors edge-curled by odorous breezes and walked on by bugs. He caught himself singing:

O Mary, we crown thee with blossoms today
Queen of the Angels
Queen of the May

Of course he would lose by this scheme a thousand other sorts of memories just as dear, would lose the grand and the fatuous baroque, mitered bishops in jewel-encrusted copes and steel-rimmed eyeglasses; but the point was not nostalgia and self-indulgence after all, no, the opposite; in fact there ought to be some way of tearing the heart completely out of the old religion, or to conceive on it something so odd that no reader would ever confuse it with the original, except that it would be as concrete, its concreteness the same concreteness (which was the point...). And what then had been that religion's heart?

What if his Jesus hadn't saved mankind?

What if the Renaissance, besides uncovering the classical past, had discovered evidence—manuscripts, documentary proofs (incontrovertible, though only after terrible struggles)—that Jesus had in the end refused to die on the cross? Had run away; had abjured his Messiah-hood; and left his followers then to puzzle that out. It would not have been out of cowardice, exactly, though the New Testaments would seem to say so, but (so the apologetic would come to run) out of a desire to share our human life completely, even our common unheroic fate. Because the true novelty, for God, would lie not in the redemption of men—an act he could perform with a millionth part of creative effort he had expended in creating the world—but in being a human being entire, growing old and impotent to redeem anybody, including himself. Something like that had happened with the false messiah Sevi in the seventeenth century: his Messiah-hood spread quickly and widely through the whole Jewish world; then, at the last minute, threatened with death, he'd converted to Islam. His followers mostly fell away, but a few still believed, and their attempts to figure out how the Messiah could act in that strange way, redeem us by not redeeming us, yielded up the Hassidic sect, with its Kabbalah and its paradoxical parables, almost Zenlike; very much what he had in mind for his church.

"A man of sorrows, and acquainted with grief"—the greatest grief, far greater than a few moments' glorious pain on that Tree. Mary's idea of it was that in the end the Father was unable to permit the death of his only-begotten son; the prophecy is Abraham and Isaac; she interceded for him, of course, her son, too, as she still intercedes for each of us. Perhaps he resented it. In any case he outlived her, and his own wife and son, too; lived on, a retired carpenter, in his daughter's house; and the rabble came before his door, and they mocked him, saying: *If thou art the Christ, take up thy cross.*

Weird! But—what made him chuckle and nearly smack his lips (in full boil now)—the thing would be, that his characters would pursue their different destinies *completely oblivious of all this oddity,* oblivious, that is, that it *is* odd; the narrative voice wouldn't notice it either; their Resurrection has always been this ambiguous one, this Refusal; their holy-card of Jesus in despised old age (after Murillo) has always marked the Sundays in their missals; their Church is just the old, the homely, the stodgy great Security, Peter's rock, which his was. His priest would venture out (bored, restless) from that security into the strange and the dangerous, at first only wishing to be a true priest, then for their own sakes, for the adventure of understanding. A nun: starting from a wild embracing of all experience, anything goes, she passes later into quietness, and, well, into habit. His wife would have to sit for that portrait, of course, of course; though she would-n't sit still. The two meet after long separation, only to pass each other at the X-point, coming from different directions, headed for different heavens—a big scene there. A saint: but which one? He or she? Well, that had always been the ques-tion; neither, or both, or one seeing at last after the other's death his sainthood, and advocating it (in the glum Vatican, a Victorian pile in Albany, the distracted Pope), a miracle awaited and given at last, unexpectedly, or not given, with-held—oh, hold on, he asked, stop a minute, slow down. He plucked out a cigarette with care. He placed his glass more exactly in the center of its cardboard coaster and arranged his change in orbits around it.

Flight over. Cats, though. He would appropriate for his Jesus that story about Muhammad called from his couch, tear-ing off his sleeve rather than disturbing the cat that had fallen asleep on it. A parable. Did Jews keep cats then? Who knows.

Oh God how subtle he would have to be, how cunning....
No paragraph, no phrase even of the thousands the book must contain could strike a discordant note, be less than fully imagined; an entire novel's worth of thought would have to be expended on each one. His attention had only to lapse for a moment, between preposition and object,

colophon and chapter heading, for dead spots to appear like gangrene that would rot the whole. Silkworms didn't work as finely or as patiently as he must, and yet boldness was all, the large stroke, the end contained in and prophesied by the beginning, the stains of his clouds infinitely various but all signifying sunrise. Unity in diversity, all that guff. An enormous weariness flew over him. The trouble with drink, he had long known, wasn't that it started up these large things but that it belittled the awful difficulties of their execution. He drank, and gazed out into the false golden day, where a passage of girl students in plaid uniforms was just then occurring, passing secret glances through the trick mirror of the window.

VI

"I'm such a chicken," the woman said to Victor. "The other day they were going around at work signing people up for the softball team. I really wanted to play. They said come on, come on, it's no big deal, it's not professional or anything...."

"Sure, just fun."

"I didn't dare."

"What's to dare? Just good exercise. Fresh air."

"Sure, *you* can say that. You've probably been playing all your life." She stabbed at the last of her ice with a stirring-stick. "I really want to, too. I'm such a chicken."

Play right field, he wanted to advise her. That had always been his retreat, nothing much ever happens in right field, you're safe there mostly unless a left-handed batter gets up, and then if you blow one, the shame is quickly forgotten. He told himself to say to her: *You should have volunteered for right field.* But his throat said it might refuse to do this, and his pleasantry could come out a muffled croak, watch out. She had finished her drink; how much time did he have to think of a thing to say to her? Buy her a drink: the sudden offer always made him feel like a masher, a cad, something antique and repellent.

"You should have volunteered for right field," he said.

"Oh, hi," she said. "How's the writing coming?"

"What?"

"The last time we talked you were writing a novel."

"Oh. Well, I sort of go in spurts." He couldn't remember still that he had ever talked with her, much less what imaginary novel he had claimed to be writing.

"It's like coming into a cave here," she said, raising her glass, empty now except for the rounded remains of ice. "You can't see anything for a while. Because of the sun in your eyes. I didn't recognize you at first." The ice she wanted couldn't escape from the bottom of the glass till she shook the glass briskly to free it; she slid a piece into her mouth then and crunched it heedlessly (a long time since he'd been able to do that) and drew her skirt away from the stool beside her, which he had come to occupy.

"Will you have another?"

"No, nope." They smiled at each other, each ready to go on with this if the other could think of something to go on with.

"So," he said.

"Taking a break?" she said. "Do you write every day?"

"Oh, no. Oh, I sort of try. I don't work very hard, really. Really I'm on vacation. All the time. Or you could say I work all the time, too. It comes to the same thing." He'd said all this before, to others; he wondered if he'd said it to her. "It's like weekend homework. Remember? There wasn't ever a time you absolutely had to do it—there was always Saturday, then Sunday—but then there wasn't ever a time when it wasn't there to do, too."

"How awful."

Sunday's dinner rich odor declining into stale leftoverhood: was it that incense that made Sunday Sunday, or what? For there was no part of Sunday that was not Sunday; even if, rebelling, you changed from Sunday suit to Saturday jeans when dinner was over, they felt not like a second skin, like a bold animal's useful hide, as they had the day before, but strange, all right but wrong to flesh chafed by wool, the flannel shirt too smooth, too indulgent after the starched white. And upstairs—though you kept as far from them as possible, that is, facedown and full-length on the parlor carpet, head inches from the funnies—the books and blue-line paper waited.

"It must take a lot of self-discipline," she said.

"Oh, I don't know. I don't have much." He felt himself about to say again, and unable to resist saying, that "Dumas, I think it was Dumas, some terrifically prolific Frenchman, said that writing novels is a simple matter—if you write one page a day, you'll write a novel a year; two pages a day, two novels a year; three pages, three novels, and so on. And how long does it take to cover a page with writing? Twenty minutes? An hour? So you see. Very easy really."

"I don't know," she said, laughing. "I can't even bring myself to write a letter."

"Oh, now *that's* hard." Easiest to leave it all just as it had been, and only inveigle into it a small sect of his own making . . . easiest of all just to leave it. It was draining from him, like the suits of the bathing beauties pictured on trick tumblers, to opposite effect. Self-indulgence only, nostalgia, pain of loss for what had not ever been worth saving: the self-indulgence of a man come to that time when the poignancy of memory is his sharpest sensation, grown sharp as the others have grown blunt. The journey now quite obviously more than half over, it had begun to lose interest; only the road already traveled still seemed full of promise. Promise! Odd word. But there it was. He blinked, and having fallen rudely silent, said: "Well, well, well."

"Well," she said. She had begun to gather up the small habitation she had made before her on the bar, purse and open wallet, folded newspaper, a single unblown rose he hadn't noticed her bring in. "I'd like to read your book sometime."

"Sure," he said. "It's not very good. I mean, it has some nice things in it, it's a good little story. But it's nothing really."

"I'm sure it's terrific." She spun the rose beneath her nose and alighted from her stool.

"I happen to have a lot of copies. I'll give you one."

"Good. Got to go."

On her way past him, she gave the rose to Victor without any other farewell. Once again sun described her long legs as she crossed the floor (sun lay on its boards like gilding, sun was impartial), and for a moment she paused, sun-blinded maybe, in the garish lozenge of real daylight made when she opened the door. Then she reappeared in the other afternoon of the window. She raised her hand in command, and a cab the color of marigolds appeared before her as though conjured. A flight of pigeons filled up the window all in an instant, seeming stationary there like a sculpted frieze, and then just as instantly didn't fill it up anymore.

"Crazy," said Victor.

"Hm?"

"Crazy broad." He gestured with the rose toward the vacant window. "My wife. You married?"

"I was. Like the pumpkin eater." Handsome guy, Victor, in a brutal, black-Irish way. Like most New York bartenders, he was really an actor, or was it the reverse?

"Divorced?"

"Separated."

He tested his thumb against the pricks of the rose. "Women. They say you got all the freedom. Then you give them their freedom, and they don't want it."

He nodded, though it wasn't wisdom that his own case would have yielded up. He was only glad now not to miss her any longer; and now and then, sad that he was glad. The last precipitate was that occasionally when a woman he'd been looking at, on a bus, in a bar, got up to leave, passing away from him for good, he felt a shooting pang of loss absurd on the face of it.

Volunteer, he thought, but for right field. And if standing there you fall into a reverie, and the game in effect goes on without you, well, you knew it would when you volunteered for the position. Only once every few innings the lost—the not-even-noticed-till-too-late—fly ball makes you sorry that things are as they are and not different, and you wonder if people think you might be bored and indifferent out there, contemptuous even, which isn't the case at all....

"On the house," Victor said, and rapped his knuckles lightly on the bar.

"Oh, hey, thanks." Kind Victor, though the glass put before him contained a powerful solvent, he knew that even as he raised the glass to his lips. He could still fly, oh, yes, always, though the cost would be terrible. But what was it he fled from? Self-indulgence, memory dearer to him than any adventure, solitude, lapidary work in his very own mines … what could be less novel, more secure? And yet it seemed dangerous; it seemed he hadn't the nerve to face it; he felt unarmed against it.

Novelty and Security: the security of novelty, the novelty of security. Always the full thing, the whole subject, the *true* subject, stood just behind the one you found yourself contemplating. The trick, but it wasn't a trick, was to take up at once the thing you saw and the reason you saw it as well; to always bite off more than you could chew, and then chew it. If it were self-indulgence for him to cut and polish his semi-precious memories, and yet seem like danger, like a struggle he was unfit for, then self-indulgence was a potent force; he must examine it, he must reckon with it.

And he would reckon with it: on that last Sunday in Advent, when his story was all told, the miracle granted or refused, the boy would lift his head from the books and blue-lined paper, the questions that had been set for him answered, and see that it had begun to snow.

Snow not falling but flying sidewise, and sudden, not signaled by the slow curdling of clouds all day and a flake or two drifting downward, but rushing forward all at once as though sent for. (The blizzard of '36 had looked like that.) And filling up the world's concavities, pillowing up in the gloaming, making night light with its whiteness and then falling still in everyone's dreams, falling for pages and pages; steepling (so an old man would dream in his daughter's house) the gaunt frame convent on the edge of town, and drifting up even to the eyes of the martyrs pictured on the sash windows of the little clapboard church, Our Lady of the Valley; the wind full of howling white riders tearing the shingles from the roof, piling the snow still higher, blizzarding the church away entirely and the convent too and all the rest of it, so that by next day oblivion whiter than the hair of God would have returned the world to normality, covering his false history and all its works in the deep ordinariness of two feet of snow; and at evening the old man in his daughter's house would sit looking out over the silent calm alone at the kitchen table, a congruence of star, cradle, season, sacament, etc., end of chapter thirty-five, the next page a flyleaf blank as snow.

The whole thing, the full thing, the step taken backward that frames the incomprehensible as in a window. *Novelty:* there was, he just then saw, a pun in the title.

He rose. Victor, lost in thought, watched the hurrying crowds that had suddenly filled the streets, afternoon gone, none with time to glance at themselves; hurrying home. One page a day, seven a week, thirty or thirty-one to the month. Fishing in his pocket for a tip, he came up with his pen, a thick black fountain pen. Fountain: it seemed less flowing, less forthcoming than that, in shape more like a bullet or a bomb.

PAN AND THE FIRE-BIRD

Sam M. Steward

First published in *Pan and the Fire-Bird*, 1930

Sam M. Steward's dialogues have a wry crispness that seems characteristic of gods and other immortals chewing the proverbial fat, and the scale of his POV is distinctly Olympian. Fire-Bird Kircp's admonishment to Pan that "Hermes was your father … even if it is not the truth you must believe it, else otherwise you shall never get into any kind of social circle" is more than just a Wildean quip or canny marketing idea. Even mythic creatures must have their myths. Because, again in Kircp's words, "All is maya, illusion," and we must all maintain our illusions if we are to be happy.

I

In those days Pan was a lonely young half-goat wandering and romping in the woods, sinking his hooves into the brown leaves and rolling over on the moss that tickled his shoulders.

Pan had one great friend, the fire-bird Kircp, whose flight through the air was a streak of flame. Kircp told Pan many things about his parents, whom Pan had never known, for when the baby goat-god opened his eyes on the world he was alone under the shade of an old apple tree.

"They were a bad lot, your parents," Kircp said, looking down his agate-colored beak, and crossing his eyes, "your mother was that wench, Kallisto, and your father ... well, that is a terrible problem. It started out to be Hermes ... uh ..."

"Do you tell me of it," Pan implored and then Kircp told him this story:

One fair day, in the Ides of the Green Grass, Kallisto bathed herself in her own pool, and her white body rising out of the dark water was like the moon rising in the sky. It was her daily practice to bathe in the pool although she, being a wood-nymph, belonged to the woods and not in the water. It was a calm day and nothing moved, except that now and then a leaf drifted slowly from a tree.

Hermes, searching for a feather that he had lost from his sandal, came upon her this day just as she left the pool. He was the color of a bronze plate since he had wintered in the south and Kallisto evidently found nothing unlovely in his sight.

But.... "What do you want?" she demanded shortly. It was always well, though difficult, to be short with young men who were the color of a bronze plate.

Hermes seized her by the arm and was all for pulling her into the bushes.

"I have something to show you," he said, and looked boldly at her.

"But doubtless I have seen it already," Kallisto whispered. "Is it yours? and is it interesting?"

Hermes laughed. "You will never find anything with which you can have more fun or that presents a more interesting phenomenon."

"What is it?" eagerly, for Kallisto was a woman.

"Curiosity has been the downfall of many an immortal," Hermes said, pulling off his sandal and holding it up. "See, it is this wing. Now if you watch it … there … when it is touched it wriggles and squirms … you can see that it is practically alive. Whenever I get ready to fly, I stroke it gently, like this"… he stroked it, top and bottom, "and it raises, it draws up, it vibrates and is ready to go. This little sandal has borne me to all manner of paradisal places and has carried me into the best circles of Olympus."

"But how very interesting," said Kallisto, "would you mind if I were to try it on?"

"Not at all," said Hermes, "and mayn't I come into your grotto while you do?"

"Certainly," said Kallisto, "you must."

Now it happened that three months later Hermes was dreadfully bored with Kallisto. "For," said he, "she goes bouncing around on my sandal so much that she has almost worn it out. I shall have to get her one of her own."

So he told Kallisto who smiled at him sweetly. "Do hurry back, my love," she said. "I am having a strange illness, but one which should be over in six months more."

Hermes laughed, and stroking his sandal, was off like a lightning flash, while Kallisto settled down at the base of her oak-tree to watch the ripples on the pool in front of her. She fell asleep.

How long she slept, she never knew, but when she awoke there was a centaur standing before her, with a lovely torso, all sun-tanned and muscled, and with glinting black eyes. But all the rest of him was horse, even to the duplication of certain things which are rarely duplicated in such malicious caricature.

Kallisto started to scream, but the centaur seized her in his arms and pressed his brown hand over her mouth.

"Quiet, hussy!" he ordered, "I'm taking you for a ride." And so saying he pressed her close to him and started to gallop off. He held her arms down close to her sides, and suddenly Kallisto felt as though Hermes were home with a new sandal and she were trying it out. And the faster the centaur rode, the weaker she became. She thought, in a blinding moment, of those terrible wood giants who join little girls to themselves while holding them high in the air. And of a sudden a thousand-pointed star of dazzling brilliance burst within her body and Kallisto went limp and fainted....

"So," said Kircp heaving a concupiscent sigh that ruffled his tail-feathers, "when you were born you were unfortunately half-horse. This scurvy attack was such a shock to your poor mother, she being in the state that she was, that it affected you. But I never could figure out how you got your goat feet."

"Well," said Pan, "I was once told of a quaint and obscure legend concerning a shepherd called Krathis and a she-goat."

Kircp pecked at Pan's haunch. "Don't let such disgraceful ideas enter your head. Hermes was your father ... even if it is not the truth you must believe it, else otherwise you shall never get into any kind of social circle."

Pan envied Kircp, suddenly, envied him his wise crossed eyes, and wished he had as long a beak as the fire-bird.

II

As Pan grew older he became as all young men, in that he felt for all young women. Now in the wood where he dwelt and romped among the brown leaves, there dwelt also a young wood-nymph who was the darling of all the satyrs and young fauns of the wood. But, with the irritating quality of all modern young women (and she *was* a modern) she would have none of any of them and worshipped Diana who was her idol, following her in the chase.

Now one day Pan came upon Syrinx as she sat in the woods re-stringing her bow.

"Your beauty," Pan said, "is like the silver bow of Diana. It is...."

Syrinx started, and looked up with wide wild eyes. She gave just a little shriek and bounded to her feet, broke through the shrubbery and ran.

"Wait!" Pan shouted after her, as he started to run, "you are like a cloud at sunrise; you are like a dove in twilight; you are ..." he tripped over a tree root and fell sprawling, but got up and continued the chase ..."like a willow tree bending over a lotus pool..." He was getting breathless and was gaining ever so little on Syrinx, who neared the river.

"O Salamacis, O Prosamachos, aid me! Deliver me from this loathsome thing!" the poor nymph cried.

The fresh gilt with which Pan had polished his hooves that day was all worn off but Pan kept up the chase.

"Now I have you!" he gasped, and leaped at Syrinx, just at the river bank. He fell, clutching her in his arms, and looked at her. By the gods! It was not she—it was only some green reeds swaying in the wind. Pan lay, disheartened, in the midst of them and sighed with self-pity. As he did, his

43

breath made a plaintive melody upon the slim stalks. "But how charming this is!" he said, astonished. "If Syrinx will not be mine in her fair body, thus, then, at least, shall I remember her."

So he took six reeds of unequal lengths and bound them together side by side and made a wind-flute, calling it a syrinx.

When he told Kircp about the affair in the evening, Kircp crossed his eyes and looked down his agate-colored beak.

"All is maya, illusion," he said wisely. "Listen to me. You know, for you have been taught, that two parallel lines can never meet.... Tell me, do you believe in perspective?"

"Perspective," said Pan, "is a worthy teaching, since by it all things appear what they are not."

"Exactly," said Kircp, "every two people are parallel lines, stretching out into space. At the end of the eye's flight they seem to come together. But you know, from your teaching, that were you at the point where vision ends, the two lines would be as far apart as ever. It all depends on perspective and the point of view. So with love. From the earth here, all sets of lines appear to converge in space, far enough out. We see two lines meet; we say 'Ah! he has merged with her, or him, as the case may be.' But he hasn't. One can never meet another except in illusion. And we are all parallel lines."

"But suppose," said Pan, "just suppose that one of them was not exactly parallel, and met another out there."

"Sh-h-h-h!" said Kircp. "Do not mention that. Such a day came once, but will never come again. It was when Hermaphroditus sprang into the pool and was seized and joined inseparably to the naiad who loved him. As their lines crossed, there was a high havoc in heaven, for after crossing they diverged out angles and clipped all the other lines in space. It was the birth of trouble and triangles and cut lines which did not extend out into space far enough to create the illusion of merging. And everyone was unhappy when they saw their lines did not merge. Luckily Zeus saw the trouble and plucked Hermaphroditus from the earth, so restoring all the lines. Now everyone, as they glance out into heaven for a reassuring look at their lines, is glad to see them so nicely merged. And they go on rejoicing. It is an illusory world, Pan."

Pan looked out at his line. "I have no maiden's line by mine, but Kircp, look; mine is next to yours! Isn't it nice! And Kircp, you can even see where we merge! I know *we* merge. I have after all been benefited by this affair; I have my syrinx of hollow reeds; I can play on it and we shall never want for food. At least I have this much. And I have learned about parallels. Kircp, aren't you happy?"

But Kircp, that wise old fire-bird, had long since fallen asleep.

III

One night when the wind was still Kircp had a vision. The next day he told Pan all about it.

"Soon," he said, "there is to be born a new god, somewhere in Palestine. As if there were not enough already without a new one coming! And he will be considered different, in that he will not believe that virtue is the performance of pleasant actions, as we do, but that virtue lies in chastity."

"But how very unnatural," said Pan.

"Yes. Now, as soon as he is born, you will not be popular. No longer will people bring wild honey and grapes to place on altars to you, or to any of the other deities. The birth of this man will be the death of the gods."

Pan was worried.

"Now I have a plan," said Kircp mysteriously, "That perhaps may prove your salvation. Of course, it will not aid the other gods. Let them die; to live in people's memories is as good as to live on Olympus."

"But what is your plan?"

"The first thing to do is send a score of brilliantly colored kites, a silver rope, and myrtle leaves as a votive offering to Æolus on his windy island, for it is necessary to have his help in this matter."

And so that night Kircp made the kites of silk and wove the ropes of silver, getting his stuffs in a strange way that frightened Pan a bit. The next morning he loaded them on his back and flew away.

At mid-day he returned, looking very successful and oily.

"Make ready," he chirped to Pan, "we have a smartish distance to go ere mid-afternoon."

Pan climbed on Kircp's broad back. "Where are we going and why?"

"What day is this?" queried Kircp.

Pan thought. "Why, it is the day of the mourning of Tammuz."

"Exactly." And try as he would, Pan could not get another word out of Kircp.

Before mid-afternoon they neared the isles of Paxos and stopped on a densely wooded island, much smaller, but close to Paxos. They rested on the top of a high cliff that looked out over the hard blue sea. In the dazzling light air small clouds hung, not chasing each other as was their usual wont.

"Did you notice anything peculiar?" asked Kircp.

Pan noticed. "There is no wind," he said.

Kircp beamed. "Æolus has tied up his every wind in his brown wind-bag. Now ... let me tell you that a ship is making from Greece to Italy and the pilot of the ship is an Egyptian by name of Thamuz ..."

But Pan could not understand.

"Well, wait, then," said Kircp, put out ever so little by Pan's stupidity.

At precisely mid-afternoon a ship hove into sight, her sails hanging loose and flappy, like the hips of a withered old crone.

"Quiet, now," warned Kircp and he prepared to listen. He had remarkable ears and had trained himself to hear things a mile away. "I have staked all on a ... verbal misinterpretation."

All afternoon the two had watched, from their point of vantage, the Paxians who were preparing an effigy of their god Tammuz to cast into the sea. But the people on this idling boat could not see them. Only Pan and Kircp saw.

Far, from the isle of Paxos, a thin wailing came and the procession started to the sea. The chant began.

"Thamous!" It was a long wail that rose in links from the isle with a crescendo in the middle.

"He hears!" cried Kircp.

"Thamous!" The birds on the little island twittered uneasily as the wail rolled over the surface of the sea.

"Thamous!" The third call rose in a welling volume.

"He answers!" Kircp whispered excitedly. "'What desire you?' he asked. Now for the crucial point."

47

The rest of the chant slid over the water and climbed the cliff.

"*Pan ... megas tethenke!*" it called, sadly mournful.

After a moment Kircp said, "It was as I planned it to be. This boat is full of travelers who are unfamiliar with the customs of this country. They misread the chant as "*Pan ho megas tethenke.*" Look! see how the people run about on the boat! They are excited. Who would not be to hear a voice call out that the great Pan is dead? Already ..." and he listened again, "... they add to it. Thamuz says that the message in its entirety read, 'When you come to Palodes, tell them that the great Pan is dead.' How very lucky that they inserted the '*ho*' between the syllables."

And it happened that on the same night the new god was born in Palestine and people accepted the announcement of the death of Pan as a divine sign. Many were the voices raised to wail the death of Pan and twelve were the voices raised to celebrate the new god. In four lands various altars were erected to the memory of Pan and long weepings attended the placing of each stone.

But still in the twilight evenings, Pan slips from out the woods and goes abroad to wander lonely in the dewy fields ... and from the marshes at midnight comes a faint sobbing ... a far-off wailing ...

MURDERER, THE HOPE OF ALL WOMEN

Oskar Kokoschka

First published in the avant-garde journal,
Der Sturm, Berlin, 1910

Translation by Stefan Rudnicki

Oskar Kokoschka was known in the early days of the twentieth century mostly for his grotesque paintings, sketches, and etchings. But as an early proponent of the Expressionist movement, he could not entertain a separation between types of expression. So he wrote plays as well. *Murderer, The Hope of All Women* is the perfect Expressionist drama, emphasizing huge emotions and unconscious urges in a monolithic, Dionysian world where only archetypes can exist. It is an effort to recreate myth, to access it directly, without literary or theatrical trappings. It is an encouragement to live the heroic life. Obscure in meaning, violent in tone, perhaps misogynistic, the images are nevertheless compelling and unforgettable.

CHARACTERS: Man
Woman
Warriors
Maidens
Old Man

The action takes place in olden days.
Night sky.
Tower with giant iron gate.
Torchlight.
A hill rising to the tower.

MAN: White face; blue armor; headband covering a wound; lead-ing the . . .

WARRIORS: Wild heads; gray and red headbands; clothes of white, black, and brown; insignias; bare legs; carrying tall torches, hand-bells.

Noise. They move slowly, arms outstretched, weary and angry. They attempt to hold the MAN back, to pull him off his horse. He continues forward unrestrained. They break the circle about him, and shout in slow crescendo. . . .

WARRIORS
We were the ring of fire around him,
We were the ring of fire around you, stormer of secret castles!

WARRIORS follow the MAN hesitantly, in a chain. He has the lead, a torch bearer by him.

WARRIORS
Lead us, White Face!

While the horse is being pulled down, MAIDENS with the leader appear on a ramp, descending from the castle wall.

WOMAN: *Red robes, golden hair asail in the wind, massive, loud.*

WOMAN
When I draw my breath, the golden disc of the sun flickers.
My eye harvests the joy of men.
Their stammering desire creeps like a beast around me.

MAIDENS break away from her, see the stranger.

FIRST MAIDEN
Our Lady!
His breath surrounds her.

FIRST WARRIOR
Our master arrives like the new day rising in the East.

SECOND MAIDEN
When will she be embraced in joy!

WOMAN
Who is this stranger who beholds me!

FIRST MAIDEN
Banished boy child of the mother of sorrows
Escaped with serpents 'round his head.
Do you recognize me?

SECOND MAIDEN
Bottomless depths shimmer.
While she drives off the welcome guest?

MAN
Did a shadow speak?
Is it you I saw? Did you see me?

WOMAN
Who is this pale stranger?
Hold him back!

FIRST MAIDEN
You've let him in. He knows our defenselessness.
The castle gate stands open wide.

FIRST WARRIOR
Whatever sails through air or swims in water,
Bears skin or feather or scale,
Hirsute or naked ghost...
Him will they all serve.

SECOND MAIDEN
Tears and laughter together furrow her golden brow.
Come, Hunter, catch us if you can....

FIRST WARRIOR
to the MAN
Embrace her!
The sound of neighing drives the mare mad.
Straddle the beast!

FIRST MAIDEN
Our Lady is lost in the web of her thoughts,
Still shapeless, unformed.

SECOND MAIDEN
Our Lady rises and falls,
But is never brought low.
THIRD MAIDEN
Our Lady is bare and soft,
But ever vigilant.

THIRD WARRIOR
Little fish caught on hook.
Fisherman reels in the she-fish.

SECOND WARRIOR
She tosses back her hair. Her face is free . . .
The spider climbs out of her web.

MAN
Who is she?

FIRST WARRIOR
She seems to fear you. Catch her!
Fear is the greatest weapon.
First frighten, then capture!

FIRST MAIDEN
Lady, let us flee.
Extinguish the lights.

SECOND MAIDEN
Mistress, let me stay and wait for the dawn. . . .
Do not ask me to go
With a longing yet in my body!

THIRD MAIDEN
He must not enter or breathe our air!
Do not let him rest here this night,
Lest he disturb our sleep.

FIRST MAIDEN
He brings no good fortune!
FIRST WARRIOR
She shows no shame!

WOMAN
Why do you bind me, Man, with your stare?
Devouring light, you confuse my flame!
All-consuming life floods over me.
Oh, take away the terrible hope—

MAN

You men! Take hot iron and burn my brand into her red flesh!

WARRIORS with torches struggle to subdue the WOMAN. An OLD MAN with an iron tears open her dress and brands her.

WOMAN
screaming in pain
Beat it back, the evil plague!

She leaps at the MAN, brandishing a knife. She wounds him in the side. The MAN falls.

WARRIORS
Exorcise him. Strike the devil dead!
Pity on us, the guiltless.
Bury the conqueror.

MAN
Senseless lust from horror to horror,
Unquenchable fumbling gyrations in the void.
Gestation without genesis, the sun collapses, space reels.
Death to those who praised me,
Oh, pitiless words.

WARRIORS
We know you not.
Spare us!
Come, you Grecian maidens, let us celebrate our wedding at his bier.

MAIDENS
He terrifies us,
While you we loved from the start.

MAIDENS lie down with WARRIORS, caressing them. Three

WARRIORS make a bier from ropes and branches, and carry the MAN on it into the tower. The MAN moves weakly. MAIDENS slam shut the gate and return to the WARRIORS.

The OLD MAN gets up and locks the gate. All becomes dark, with a little light emerging from behind the gate, the MAN's cage.

WOMAN
He cannot live. He cannot die.
He is pale as a ghost.

She moves in a circle around the tower, grabs the gate, rattling it with desperation.

WOMAN
Open the gate! I must go to him.

WARRIORS and MAIDENS
variously, in confusion and shadow
We have lost the key—we'll find it—Don't you have it?—Did you see it?—It's not our fault—Who are you?—What are you?—The struggle is unexplainable, and will last forever.

A cock crows. First flash of dawn. WOMAN reaches through the gate, panting.

WOMAN
White Face! Are you afraid?
Are you sleeping? Awake? Can you hear me?

MAN
raising himself slowly, singing, in a trance
Wind sighs, time on time,
Solitude, peace, and desire confuse me.
Worlds swing by, no air, night draws to its end.

WOMAN
laughing, her body quivering
So much life pours from the wound,
So much force lost through the gate,
He is pale as a corpse.

The MAN is now standing, leaning on the gate.

WOMAN
Here in this cage I tame a wild beast.
Does your song howl with desire?

The MAN opens his mouth to speak. A cock crows.

WOMAN
shivering
You . . . you are not dying?

MAN
with power
Stars and moon! Woman!
A singing angel, shining bright,
In my dream or awake, I saw.
My breath unravels the darkness.
Mother. . . . You left me here.

The WOMAN lies on him, upright, separated by the gate. She slowly opens it to him.

WOMAN
Forget me not . . .

MAN
Corroding thoughts melt the mind . . .

WOMAN
Your wife!

MAN
A shy sliver of light . . .

WOMAN
Man! Dream for me . . .

MAN
Peace, peace. Delusion, leave me . . .

WOMAN opens her mouth to speak.

MAN
I am afraid.

WOMAN
with increasing violence, screaming
I don't want to let you live. You!
You weaken me—
I kill you, and you bind me!
I capture you, and you hold me!
Let go of me—you clasp me as iron—
Chained—away—help!
I lost the key that held you.

*WOMAN lets go of the gate, collapses. The MAN stands erect,
tears down the gate, touches the WOMAN, with fingers of his
outstretched hand. She rears up stiffly in violent spasm, white
now. She feels her end is near, tenses her limbs, then loosens them
in a slowly descending scream. The WOMAN collapses, seizing
a torch for the OLD MAN. The torch goes out in a shower of
sparks. The MAN stands on the top step. WARRIORS and MAID-
ENS run screaming.*

WARRIORS and MAIDENS
The Devil!

Bind him!
Save yourselves,
Each for himself!
We are lost!

The MAN steps forward, killing them like flies. Flames leap over the tower, and rip it open from top to bottom. There is a path between the flames, through which the MAN departs.

Far, far away, a cock crows.

THE TOUCH OF PAN

Algernon Blackwood

First published in the second decade of the twentieth century

Blackwood, who published numerous collections of myth-based horror in the years between 1906 and 1923, was an Englishman who traveled extensively, even serving a term as a reporter for *The New York Times*. H.P. Lovecraft called him "the one absolute and unquestioned master of weird atmosphere...." To quote further, "Above all others he understands how fully some sensitive minds dwell forever on the borderland of dream, and how relatively slight is the distinction betwixt those images formed from actual objects and those excited by the play of the imagination." With "The Touch of Pan," as with most of Blackwood's stories, we are convinced that there is a world just beyond ours, and much more interesting, where mythical beings live and flourish and laugh at us in our sad and trivial pursuits.

I

An idiot, Heber understood, was a person in whom intelligence had been arrested—instinct acted, but not reason. A lunatic, on the other hand, was someone whose reason had gone awry—the mechanism of the brain was injured. The lunatic was out of relation with his environment; the idiot had merely been delayed *en route.*

Be that as it might, he knew at any rate that a lunatic was not to be listened to, whereas an idiot—well, the one he fell in love with certainly had the secret of some instinctual knowledge that was not only joy, but a kind of sheer natural joy. Probably it was that sheer natural joy of living that reason argues to be untaught, degraded. In any case—at thirty—he married her instead of the daughter of a duchess he was engaged to. They lead today that happy, natural, vagabond life called idiotic, unmindful of that world the majority of reasonable people live only to remember.

Though born into an artificial social clique that made it difficult, Heber had always loved the simple things. Nature, especially, meant much to him. He would rather see a woodland misty with bluebells than all the châteaux on the Loire; the thought of a mountain valley in the dawn made his feet lonely in the grandest houses. Yet in these very houses was his home established. Not that he underestimated worldly things—their value was too obvious—but that it was another thing he wanted. Only he did not know precisely *what* he wanted until this particular idiot made it plain.

Her case was a mild one, possibly; the title bestowed by implication rather than by specific motion. Her family did not say that she was imbecile or half-witted, but that she was "not all there" they probably did say. Perhaps she saw men as trees walking, perhaps she saw through a glass darkly. . . . Heber, who had met her once or twice, though never yet to speak to, did not analyze her degree of sight, for in him, personally, she woke a secret joy and wonder that almost involved a touch of awe. The part of her that was "not all there" dwelt in an "elsewhere" that he longed to know about. He wanted to share it with her. She seemed aware of certain happy and desirable things that reason and too much thinking hid.

He just felt this instinctively without analysis. The values they set upon the prizes of life were similar. Money to her was just stamped metal, fame a loud noise of sorts, position nothing. Of people she was aware as a dog or bird might be aware—they were kind or unkind. Her parents, having collected much metal and achieved position, proceeded to make a loud noise of sorts with some success; and since she did not contribute, either by her appearance or her tastes, to their ambitions, they neglected her and made excuses. They were ashamed of her existence. Her father in particular justified Nietzsche's shrewd remark that no one with a loud voice can listen to subtle thoughts.

She was, perhaps, sixteen; for, though she did not look it, eighteen or nineteen was probably more in accord with her birth certificate. Her mother was content, however, that she should dress the lesser age, preferring to tell strangers that she was childish, rather than admit that she was backward.

"You'll never marry at all, child, much less marry as you might," she said, "if you go on about with that rabbit expression on your face. That's not the way to catch a nice young man of the sort we get down to stay with us now. Many a chorus girl with less than you've got has caught them easily enough. Your sister's done well. Why not do the same? There's nothing to be shy or frightened about."

"But I'm not shy or frightened, Mother. I'm bored. I mean *they* bore me."

It made no difference to the girl; she was herself. The bored expression in the eyes—the rabbit, not-all-there expression—gave place sometimes to another look. Yet not often, nor with anybody. It was this other look that stirred the strange joy in the man who fell in love with her. It was not easily described. It was very wonderful. Whether sixteen or nineteen, she then looked—a thousand.

The house party was of that up-to-date kind prevalent in Heber's world. Husbands and wives were not asked together. There was a cynical disregard of the decent (not the stupid) conventions that savored of abandon, perhaps of decadence. He only went himself in the hope of seeing the backward daughter once again. Her millionaire parents afflicted him, the smart folk tired him. Their peculiar affectation of a special language, their strange belief that they were of importance, their treatment of the servants, their calculated self-indulgence, all jarred upon him more than usual. At bottom he heartily despised the whole vapid set. He felt uncomfortable and out of place. Though not a prig, he abhorred the way these folk believed themselves the climax of fine living. Their open immorality disgusted him, their indiscriminate lovemaking was merely nasty; he watched the very girl he was at last to settle down with behaving as the tone of the clique expected over her final fling—and, bored by the strain of so much "modernity," he tried to get away. Tea was long over, the sunset interval invited, he felt hungry for trees and fields that were not self-conscious— and he escaped. The flaming June day was turning chill. Dusk hovered over the ancient house, veiling the pretentious new wing that had been added. And he came across the idiot girl at the bend of the drive, where the birch trees shivered in the evening wind. His heart gave a sudden leap.

She was leaning against one of the dreadful statues—it was a satyr—that sprinkled the lawn. Her back was to him; she gazed at a group of broken pine trees in the park beyond. He paused an instant, then went on quickly, while his mind scurried, to recall her name. They were within easy speaking range.

"Miss Elizabeth!" he cried, yet not too loudly, lest she might vanish as suddenly as she had appeared. She turned at once. Her eyes and lips were smiling welcome at him without pretence. She showed no surprise.

"You're the first of the lot who's said it properly," she exclaimed, as he came up. "Everyone calls me Elizabeth instead of Elspeth. It's idiotic. They don't even take the trouble to get a name right."

"It is," he agreed, "quite idiotic." He did not correct her. Possibly he had said Elspeth after all—the names were similar. Her perfectly natural voice was grateful to his ear, and soothing. He looked at her all over with an open admiration that she noticed and, without concealment, liked. She was very untidy, the gray stockings on her slim, vigorous legs were torn, her short skirt was spattered with mud. Her nut-brown hair, glossy and plentiful, flew loose about her neck and shoulders. In place of the usual belt she had tied a colored handkerchief around her waist. She wore no hat. What she had been doing to get in such a state, while her parents entertained a "distinguished" party, he did not know, but it was not difficult to guess. Climbing trees or riding bareback and astride was probably the truth. Yet her disheveled state became her well, and the welcome in her face delighted him. She remembered him, she was glad. He, too, was glad, and a sense both happy and reckless stirred in his heart. "Like a wild animal," he said, "you come out at dusk—"

"To play with my kind," she answered in a flash, throwing him a glance of invitation that made his blood go dancing.

He leaned against the statue a moment, asking himself why this young Cinderella of a parvenu family delighted him when all the London beauties left him cold. There was a lift through his whole being as he watched her, slim and supple, grace shining through the untidy modern garb—almost as though she wore no clothes. He thought of a panther standing upright. Her poise was so alert—one arm upon the marble ledge, one leg bent across the other, the hip-line showing like a bird's curved wing. Wild animal or bird, flashed across his mind; something untamed and natural. Another second and she might leap away—or spring into his arms.

It was a deep, delicious sensation in him that produced the mental picture. "Pure and natural," a voice whispered with it in his heart, "as surely as *they* are just the other thing!" And the thrill struck with unerring aim at the very root of that unrest he had always known in the start of life to which he was called. She made the natural clean and pure. This girl and himself were somehow kin. The primitive thing broke loose in him.

In two seconds, while he stood with her beside the vulgar statue, these thoughts passed through his mind. But he did not at first give utterance to any of them. He spoke more formally, although laughter, due to his happiness, lay close behind.

"They haven't asked you to the party, then? Or you don't care about it? Which is it?"

"Both," she said, looking fearlessly into his face. "But I've been waiting here ten minutes already. Why were you so long?"

This outspoken honesty was hardly what he expected, yet in another sense he was not surprised. Her eyes were very penetrating, very innocent, very frank. He felt her as clean and sweet as some young fawn that asks plainly to be stroked and fondled. He told the truth: "I couldn't get away before. I had to play about and—" when she interrupted with impatience:

"*They* don't want you," she exclaimed scornfully. "I do."

And, before he could choose one out of the several answers that rushed into his mind, she nudged him with her foot, holding it out a little so that he saw the shoelace was unfastened. She nodded her head toward it, and pulled her skirt up half an inch as he at once stooped down.

"And, anyhow," she went on as he fumbled with the lace, touching her ankle with his hand, "you're going to marry one of them. I read it in the paper. You'll be miserable. It's idiotic."

The blood rushed to his head, but whether owing to his stooping or to something else, he could not say.

"I only came—I only accepted," he said quickly, "because I wanted to see you again."

"Of course. I made Mother ask you."

He did an impulsive thing. Kneeling as he was, he bent his head a little lower and suddenly kissed the soft gray stocking—then stood up and looked her in the face. She was laughing happily, no sign of embarrassment in her anywhere, no trace of outraged modesty. She only looked very pleased.

"I've tied a knot that won't come undone in a hurry—" he began, then stopped dead. For as he said it, gazing into her smiling face, another expression looked forth at him from the two big eyes of hazel. Something rushed from his heart to meet it. It may have been that playful kiss, it may have been the way she took it; but, at any rate, there was a strength in the new emotion that made him unsure of who he was and of whom he looked at. He forgot the place, the time, his own identity and hers. . . . The lawn swept from beneath his feet, the English sunset with it. He forgot his host and hostess, his fellow guests, even his father's name and his own in the bargain. He was carried away upon a great tide, the girl always beside him. He left the shoreline in the distance, already half-forgotten, the shoreline of his education, learning, manners, social point of view—everything to which his father had most carefully brought him up as the scion of an old established English family. This girl had torn up the anchor. Only the anchor had previously been loosened a little, perhaps, by his own unconscious and restless efforts. . . .

Where was she taking him to? Upon what island would they land. . .?

"I'm younger than you—a good deal," she broke in upon his rushing mood. "But that doesn't matter a bit, does it? We're about the same age really."

With the happy sound of her voice the extraordinary sensation passed—or, rather, it became normal. But that it lasted an appreciable time was proved by the fact that they had left the statue on the lawn, the house was no longer visible behind them, and they were now walking side by side between the massive rhododendron clumps. They brought up against a five-barred gate into the park. They leaned upon the topmost bar, and he felt her shoulder touching his—edging into it—as they looked across to the grove of pines.

"I feel absurdly young," he said without a sign of affectation, "and yet I've been looking for you a thousand years and more."

The afterglow lit up her face; it fell on her loose hair and tumbled blouse, turning them amber red. She looked not only soft and comely, but extraordinarily beautiful. The strange expression haunted the deep eyes again, the lips were a little parted, the young breast heaving slightly, joy and excitement in her presentment. And as he watched her he knew that all he had just felt was due to her close presence, her atmosphere, her perfume, her physical warmth and vigor. It emanated directly from her being.

"Of course," she said, and laughed so that he felt her breath upon his face. He bent lower to bring his own on a level, gazing straight into her eyes that were still fixed upon the field beyond. They were clear and luminous as pools of water, and in their center, sharp as a photograph, he saw the reflection of the pine grove, perhaps a hundred yards away. With detailed accuracy he saw it, empty and motionless in the glimmering June dusk.

Then something caught his eye. He examined the picture more closely. He drew slightly nearer. He almost touched her face with his own, forgetting for a moment whose were the eyes that served him for a mirror. For, looking intently thus, it seemed to him that there was movement, a passing to and fro, a stirring as of figures among the trees. . . . Then suddenly the entire picture was obliterated. She had dropped her lids. He heard her speaking—the warm breath was again upon her face:

"In the heart of that wood dwell I."

His heart gave another leap—more violent than the first—for the sentence caught him like a spell. There was a lilt and rhythm in the words, a wonder and a beauty, that made it poetry. She laid emphasis upon the pronoun and the nouns. It seemed the last line of some delicious runic verse:

"In the *heart* of that *wood*—dwell *I*..."

And it flashed across him: that living, moving, inhabited pine wood was her thought. It was thus she thought it, saw it. Her nature flung back to a life she understood, a life that needed, claimed her. The ostentatious and artificial values that surrounded her she denied, even as the distinguished house party of her ambitious, masquerading family neglected her. Of course she was unnoticed by them—just as a swallow or a wild rose were unnoticed.

He knew her secret then, for she had told it to him. It was his own secret too. They were akin, as the birds and animal were akin. They belonged together in some free and open life, natural, wild, untamed. That unhampered life was flowing about them now, rising, beating with delicious tumult in her veins and his, yet innocent as the sunlight and the wind—because it was as freely recognized.

"Elspeth!" he cried, "come, take me with you! We'll go at once. Come—hurry—before we forget to be happy, or remember to be wise again—!"

His words stopped halfway toward completion, for a perfume floated past him, born of the summer dusk, perhaps, yet sweet with a penetrating magic that made his senses reel with some remembered joy. No flower, no scented garden bush delivered it. It was the perfume of young, spendthrift life, sweet with the purity that reason had not yet stained. The girl moved closer. Gathering her loose hair between her fingers, she brushed his cheeks and eyes with it, her slim, warm body pressing against him as she leaned over laughingly:

"In the hour of darkness," she whispered in his ear; *"when the moon puts the house upon the statue!"*

And he understood. Her world lay behind the vulgar, staring day. He turned. He heard the flutter of skirts—just caught the gray stockings, swift and light, as they flew behind the rhododendron masses. And she was gone.

He stood a long time, leaning upon that five-barred gate.... It was the dressing gong that recalled him at length to what seemed the present. By the conservatory door, as he went slowly in, he met his distinguished cousin—who was helping the girl he himself was to marry to enjoy her "final fling." He looked at his cousin. He realized suddenly that he was merely vicious. There was no sun and wind, no flowers— there was depravity only, lust instead of laughter, excitement in place of happiness. It was calculated, not spontaneous. His mind was in it. Without joy it was. He was not natural.

"Not a girl in the whole lot fit to look at," his cousin exclaimed with peevish boredom, excusing himself stupidly for his illicit conduct. "I'm off in the morning." He shrugged his blue-blooded shoulders. "These millionaires! Their shooting's all right, but their mixum–gatherum weekends—bah!" His gesture completed all he had to say about this one in particular. He glanced sharply, nastily, at his companion. "*You* look as if you'd found something!" he added, with a suggestive grin. "Or have you seen the ghost that was paid for with the house?" And he guffawed and let his eyeglass drop. "Lady Hermione will be asking for an explanation—eh?"

"Idiot!" replied Heber, and ran upstairs to dress for dinner.

But the word was wrong, he remembered, as he closed his door. It was lunatic he had meant to say, yet something more as well. He saw the smart, modern philanderer somehow as a beast.

II

It was nearly midnight when he went up to bed, after an evening of intolerable amusement. The abandoned moral attitude, the common rudeness, the contempt of all others but themselves, the ugly jests, the horseplay of tasteless minds that passed for gaiety, above all the shamelessness of the women that behind the cover of fine breeding aped emancipation, afflicted him to a boredom that touched desperation.

He understood now with a clarity unknown before. As with his cousin, so with these. They took life, he saw, with a brazen effrontery they thought was freedom, while yet it was life that they denied. He felt vampired and degraded; spontaneity went out of him. The fact that the geography of bedrooms was studied openly seemed an affirmation of vice that sickened him. Their ways were nauseous merely. He escaped—unnoticed.

He locked his door, went to the open window, and looked out into the night—then started. For silver dressed the lawn and park, the shadow of the building lay dark across the elaborate garden, and the moon, he noticed, was just high enough to put the house upon the statue. The chimney stacks edged the pedestal precisely.

"Odd!" he exclaimed. "Odd that I should come at the very moment—!" then smiled as he realized how his proposed adventure would be misinterpreted, its natural innocence and spirit ruined—if he were seen. "And someone would be sure to see me on a night like this. There are couples still hanging about in the garden." And he glanced at the shrubberies and secret paths that seemed to float upon the warm June air like islands.

He stood for a moment framed in the glare of the electric light, then turned back into the room; and at that instant a low sound like a birdcall rose from the lawn below. It was soft and flutey, as though someone played two notes upon a reed, a piping sound. He had been seen, and she was waiting for him. Before he knew it, he had made an answering call, of oddly similar kind, then switched the light out.

Three minutes later, dressed in simpler clothes, with a cap pulled over his eyes, he reached the back lawn by means of the conservatory and billiard room. He paused a moment to look about him. There was no one, although the lights were still ablaze. "I am an idiot," he chuckled to himself. "I'm acting on instinct!" He ran.

The sweet night air bathed him from head to foot; there was strength and cleansing in it. The lawn shone wet with dew. He could almost smell the perfume of the stars. The fumes of wine, cigars, and artificial scent were left behind, the atmosphere exhaled by civilization, by heavy thoughts, by bodies overdressed, unwisely stimulated—all, all forgotten. He passed into a world of magical enchantment. The hush of the open sky came down. In black and white the garden lay, brimmed full with beauty, shot by the ancient silver of the moon, spangled with the stars' old gold. And the night wind rustled in the rhododendron masses as he flew between them.

In a moment he was beside the statue, engulfed now by the shadow of the building, and the girl detached herself silently from the blur of darkness. Two arms were flung about his neck, a shower of soft hair fell on his cheek with a heady scent of earth and leaves and grass, and the same instant they were away together at full speed—toward the pine wood. Their feet were soundless on the soaking grass.

They went so swiftly that they made a whir of following wind that blew her hair across his eyes.

And the sudden contrast caused a shock that put a blank, perhaps, upon his mind, so that he lost the standard of remembered things. For it was no longer merely a particular adventure; it seemed a habit and a natural joy resumed.

It was not new. He realized the momentum of an accustomed happiness, mislaid, it may be, but certainly familiar. They sped across the gravel paths that intersected the well-groomed lawn, they leaped the flowerbeds, so laboriously shaped in mockery, they clambered over the ornamental iron railings, scorning the easier five-barred gate in the park. The longer grass then shook the dew in soaking showers against his knees. He stooped, as though in some foolish effort to turn up something, then realized that his legs, of course, were bare. *Her* garment was already high and free, for she, too, was barelegged like himself. He saw her little ankles, wet and shining in the moonlight, and flinging himself down, he kissed them happily, plunging his face into the dripping, perfumed grass. Her ringing laughter mingled with his own, as she stooped beside him the same instant; her hair hung in a silver cloud; her eyes gleamed through its curtain into his; then, suddenly, she soaked her hands in the heavy dew and passed them over his face with a softness that was like the touch of some scented southern wind.

"Now you are anointed with the Night," she cried. "No one will know you. You are forgotten of the world. Kiss me!"

"We'll play forever and ever," he cried, "the eternal game that was old when still the world was young," and lifting her in his arms he kissed her eyes and lips. There was some natural bliss of song and dance laughter in his heart, an elemental bliss that caught them together as wind and sunlight catch the branches of a tree. She leaped from the ground to meet his swinging arms, and in an instant was upon his shoulders. He ran with her, then tossed her off and caught her neatly as she fell. Evading a second capture, she danced ahead, holding out one shining arm that he might follow. Hand in hand they raced on together through the clean summer moonlight. Yet there remained a smooth softness as of fur against his neck and shoulders, and he saw then that she wore skins of tawny color that clung to her body closely, that he wore them too, and that her skin, like his own, was of a sweet dusky brown.

Then, pulling her toward him, he stared into her face. She suffered the close gaze a second, but no longer, for with a burst of sparkling laughter again she leaped into his arms, and before he shook her free she had pulled and tweaked the two small horns that hid in the thick curly hair behind, and just above, the ears.

And that willful tweaking turned him wild and reckless. That touch ran down him deep into the mothering earth. He leaped and ran and sang with a great laughing sound. The wine of eternal youth flushed all his veins with joy, and the old, old world was young again with every impulse of natural happiness intensified with the Earth's own foaming tide of life.

From head to foot he tingled with the delight of spring, prodigal with creative power. Of course he could fly the bushes and fling wild across the open! Of course the wind and moonlight fitted close and soft about him like a skin! Of course he had youth and beauty for playmates, with dancing, laughter, singing, and a thousand kisses! For he and she were natural once again. They were free together of those long-forgotten days when "Pan leaped through the roses in the months of June...!"

With the girl swaying this way and that upon his shoulders, tweaking his horns with mischief and desire, hanging her flying hair before his eyes, then bending swiftly over again to lift it, he danced to join the rest of their companions in the little moonlit grove of pines beyond....

III

They rose somewhat pointed, perhaps, against the moonlight those English pines—more with the shape of cypresses, some might have thought. A stream gushed down between their roots, there were mossy ferns, and rough gray boulders with lichen on them. But there was no dimness, for the silver of the moon sprinkled freely through the branches like the faint sunlight that it really was, and the air ran out to meet them with a heady fragrance that was wiser far than wine.

The girl, in an instant, was whirled from her perch on his shoulders and caught by a dozen arms that bore her into the heart of the merry, careless throng. Whisht! Whew! Whir! She was gone, but another, fairer still, was in her place, with skin as soft and knees that clung as tightly. Her eyes were liquid amber, grapes hung between her little breasts, her arms entwined about him, smoother than marble, and as cool. She had a crystal laugh.

But he flung her off, so that she fell plump among a group of bigger figures lolling against a twisted root and roaring with a jollity that boomed like wind through the chorus of a song. They seized her, kissed her, then sent her flying. They were happier, after all, with their glad singing. They held stone goblets, red and foaming in their broad-palmed hands.

"The mountains lie behind us!" cried someone dancing past. "We are come at last into our valley of delight. Grapes, breasts, and rich red lips! Ho! Ho! It is time to press them that the juice of life may run!" The figure waved a cluster of ferns across the air and vanished amid a cloud of song and laughter.

"It is ours. Use it!" answered a deep, ringing voice. "The valleys are our own. No climbing now!" And a wind of echoing cries gave answer from all sides. "Life! Life! Life! Abundant, flowing over—use it, use it!"

A troop of nymphs rushed forth, escaped from clustering arms and lips they yet openly desired. He chased them in and out among the waving branches, while she who had brought him ever followed, and sped past him and away again. He caught three gleaming soft brown bodies, then fell beneath them, smothered, bubbling with joyous laughter— next freed himself and, while they sought to drag him captive again, escaped and raced with a leap upon a slimmer, sweeter outline that swung up—only just in time upon a lower bough, whence she leaned down above him with hanging net of hair and merry eyes. A few feet beyond his reach, she laughed and teased him—the one who brought him in, the one he ever sought, and who forever sought him too....

It became a riotous glory of wild children who romped and played with an impassioned glee beneath the moon. For the world was young and they, her happy offspring, glowed with the life she poured so freely into them. All intermingled, the laughing voices rose into a foam of song that broke against the stars. The difficult mountains had been climbed and were forgotten. Good! Then, enjoy the luxuriant, fruitful valley and be glad! And glad they were, brimful with spontaneous energy, natural as birds and animals that obeyed the big, deep rhythm of a simpler age—natural as wind and innocent as sunshine.

Yet, for all the untamed riot, there was a lift of beauty pulsing underneath. Even when the wildest abandon approached the heat of orgy, when the reckless appeared excess—there hid that marvelous touch of loveliness which makes the natural sacred. There was coherence, purpose, the fulfilling of an exquisite law: and—there was worship. The form it took, happily, was strange as well as riotous, yet in its strangeness dreamed innocence and purity, and in its very riot flamed that spirit which is divine.

For he found himself at length beside her once again; breathless and panting, her sweet brown limbs aglow from the excitement of escape denied; eyes shining like a blaze of stars, and pulses beating with tumultuous life—helpless and yielding against the strength that pinned her down between the roots. His eyes put mastery on her own. She looked up into his face, obedient, happy, soft with love, surrendering with the same delicious abandon that had swept her for a moment into other arms. "You caught me in the end," she sighed. "I only played awhile."

"I hold you forever," he replied, half-wondering at the rough power in his voice.

It was here the hush of worship stole upon her little face, into her obedient eyes, about her parted lips. She ceased her willful struggling.

"Listen!" she whispered. "I hear a step upon the glades beyond. The iris and the lily open; the Earth is ready, waiting; we must be ready too!" "*He* is coming!"

He released her and sprang up; the entire company rose too. All stood, all bowed the head. There was an instant subtle panic, but it was the panic of reverent awe that preludes a descent of deity. For a wind passed through the branches with a sound that is the oldest in the world and so the youngest. Above it there rose the shrill, faint piping of a little reed. . . .

Only the first, true sounds were audible—wind and water: the tinkling of the dewdrops as they fell, the murmur of the tree against the air. This was the piping that they heard. And in the hush the stars bent down to hear, the riot paused, the orgy passed and died. The figures waited, kneeling then with one accord. They listened with—the Earth.

"He comes. . . . He comes. . . ." the valley breathed about them.

A footfall from far away came treading across a world unruined and unstained. It fell with the wind and water, sweetening the valley into life as it approached. Across the rivers and forests it came gently, tenderly, but swiftly and with a power that knew majesty.

"He comes. . . . He comes. . . ." rose with the murmur of the wind and water from the host of lowered heads.

The footfall came nearer, treading a world grown soft with worship. It reached the grove. It entered. There was a sense of intolerable loveliness, of brimming life, of rapture. The thousand faces lifted like a cloud. They heard the piping close. . . . And so He came.

But He came with blessing. With the stupendous Presence there was joy, the joy of abundant, natural life, pure as the sunlight and the wind. He passed among them. There was great movement—as of a forest shaking, as of deep water falling, as of a cornfield swaying to the wind, gentle as of a harebell shedding its burden of dew that it has held too long because of love. He passed among them, touching every head. The great hand swept with tenderness each face, lingered a moment on each beating heart. There was sweetness, peace, and loveliness; but above all, there was—life. He sanctioned every natural joy in them and blessed each passion with his power of creation.... Yet each one saw him differently: some as a wife or maiden desired with fire, some as a youth or stalwart husband, others as a figure veiled with stars or cloaked in luminous mist, hardly attainable; others, again—the fewest these, not more than two or three—as that mysterious wonder which tempts the heart away from known familiar sweetness into a wilderness of undecipherable magic without flesh and blood.

To two, in particular, He came so near that they could feel his breath of hills and fields upon their eyes. He touched them with both mighty hands. He stroked the marble breasts, He felt the little hidden horns ... and as they bent lower so that their lips met together for an instant, He took her arms and twined them about the curved, brown neck that she might hold him closer still....

Again a footfall sounded far away upon an unruined world ... and He was gone—back into the wind and water whence He came. The thousand faces lifted; all stood up, the hush of worship still among them. There was a quiet as of the dawn. The piping floated over the woods and fields, fading into silence. All looked at one another.... And then once more the laughter and the play broke loose.

IV

"We'll go," she cried, "and peep upon that other world where life hangs like a prison on their eyes!"

And, in a moment, they were across the soaking grass, the lawn and flowerbeds, and close to the walls of the heavy mansion. He peered in through a window, lifting her up to peer in with him. He recognized the world to which he outwardly belonged; he understood; a little gasp escaped him; and a slight shiver ran down the girl's body into his own. She turned her eyes away. "See," she murmured in his ear, "it's ugly, it's not natural. They feel guilty and ashamed. There is no innocence!" She saw the men; it was the women that he saw chiefly.

Lolling ungracefully, with a kind of boldness that asserted independence, the women smoked their cigarettes with an air of invitation they sought to conceal and yet plainly showed. He saw his familiar world in nakedness. Their backs were bare, for all their elaborate clothes they wore; they hung their breasts uncleanly; in their eyes shone light that had never known the open sun. Hoping they were alluring and desirable, they feigned a guilty ignorance of that hope. They all pretended. Instead of wind and dew upon their hair, he saw flowers grown artificially to ape wild beauty, tresses without luster borrowed from the slums of city factories. He watched them maneuvering with the men; heard dark sentences; caught gestures half delivered whose meaning should just convey that glimpse of guilt they deemed to increase pleasure. The women were calculating, but nowhere glad; the men experienced, but nowhere joyous. Pretended innocence lay cloaked with a veil of something that whispered secretly, clandestine, ashamed, yet with a brazen air that laid mockery instead of sunshine in their smiles. Vice masquer-aded in the ugly shape of pleasure; beauty was degraded into calculated tricks. They were not natural. They knew not joy.

"The forward ones, they are civilized!" she laughed in his ear, tweaking his horns with energy. "*We* are the backward!"

"Unclean," he muttered, recalling a catchword of the world he gazed upon.

They were the civilized! They were refined and edu-cated—advanced. Generations of careful breeding, mate cau-tiously selecting mate, laid the polish of caste upon their hands and faces where gleamed ridiculous, untaught jew-els—rings, bracelets, necklaces hanging absurdly from every possible angle.

"But—they are dressed up—for fun!" he exclaimed, more to himself than to the girl in the skins who clung to his shoul-der with her naked arms.

"*Un*dressed!" she answered, putting her brown hand in play across his eyes. "Only they have forgotten even that!" And another shiver passed through her into him. He turned and hid his face against the soft skins that touched his cheek. He kissed her body. Seizing his horns, she pressed him to her, laughing happily.

"Look!" she whispered, raising her head again. "They're coming out." And he saw that two of them, a man and a girl, with an interchange of secret glances, had stolen from the room and were already by the door of the conservatory that led into the garden. It was wife to be—and his distinguished cousin.

"Oh, Pan!" she cried in mischief. The girl sprang from his arms and pointed. "We will follow them. We will put natural life into their little veins!"

"Or panic terror," he answered, catching the yellow panther skin and following her swiftly 'round the building. He kept in the shadow, though she ran full into the blaze of moonlight. "But they can't see us," she called, looking over her shoulder a moment. "They can only feel our presence, perhaps." And, as she danced across the lawn, it seemed a moonbeam slipped from a sapling birch tree that the wind curved earthwards, then tossed back against the sky.

Keeping just ahead, they led the pair, by methods known instinctively to elemental blood yet not translatable—led them towards the little grove of waiting pines. The night wind murmured in the branches; a bird woke into a sudden burst of song. These sounds were plainly audible. But four little pointed ears caught other, wilder, notes behind the wind and music of the bird—the cries and ringing laughter, the leaping footsteps and the happy singing of their merry kin within the wood.

And the throng paused then amid the revels to watch the "civilized" draw near. They presently reached the trees, halted, looked about them, hesitated a moment—then, with a hurried movement as of shame and fear lest they be caught, entered the zone of shadow.

"Let's go in here," said the man, without the music in his voice. "It's dry on the pine needles, and we can't be seen." He led the way; she picked up her skirts and followed over the strip of long wet grass. "Here's a log all ready for us," he added, sat down, and drew her into his arms with a sigh of satisfaction. "Sit on my knee; it's warmer for your pretty figure." He chuckled; evidently they were on familiar terms, for though she hesitated there was no real resistance in her, and she allowed the ungraceful roughness. "But are we *quite* safe? Are you sure?" she asked between his kisses.

"What does it matter, even if we're not?" he replied, establishing her more securely on his knees. "But, as a matter of fact, we're safer here than in my own house." He kissed her hungrily. "By Jove, Hermione, but you're divine," he cried passionately, "divinely beautiful. I love you with every atom of my being—with my very soul."

"Yes, dear, I know—I mean, I know you do, but—"

"But what?" he asked impatiently.

"Those horrid detectives—"

He laughed. Yet it seemed to annoy him. "My wife *is* a beast, isn't she—to have me watched like that," he said quickly.

"They're everywhere," she replied, a sudden hush in her tone. She looked at the encircling trees a moment, then added bitterly: "I hate her, simply *hate* her for it."

"I love you," he cried, crushing her to him, "that's all that matters now. Don't let's waste time talking about the rest." She contrived to shudder, and hid her face against his coat, while he showered kisses on her neck and hair.

And the solemn pine trees watched them, the silvery moonlight fell on their faces, the scent of new-mown hay went floating past.

"I love you with my very soul," he repeated with intense conviction. "I'd do anything, give up anything, bear anything—just to give you a moment's happiness. I swear it—before God!"

There was a faint sound among the trees behind them, and the girl sat up, alert. She would have scrambled to her feet, but that he held her tight.

"What the devil's the matter with you tonight?" he asked in a different tone, his vexation plainly audible. "You're as nervy as if *you* were being watched, instead of me."

She paused before she answered, her finger on her lips. Then she spoke slowly, hushing her voice a little:

"Watched!" she repeated. "That's exactly what I did feel. I've felt ever since we came into the wood."

"Nonsense, Hermione. It's too many cigarettes." He drew her back into his arms, forcing her head up so that he could kiss her better.

"I suppose it is nonsense," she said, smiling. "It's gone now, anyhow."

He began admiring her hair, her dress, her shoes, her pretty ankles, while she resisted in a way that proved her practice. "It's not *me* you love," she pouted, yet drinking in his praise. She listened to his repeated assurances that he loved her with his "soul" and was prepared for any sacrifice.

"I feel so safe with you," she murmured, knowing the moves in the game as well as he did. She looked up guiltily into his face, while he looked down with a passion that he thought perhaps was joy.

"You'll be married before the summer's out," he said, "and all the thrill and excitement will be over. Poor Hermione!" She lay back in his arms, drawing his face down with both hands, and kissing him on the lips. "You'll have more of him than you can do with—eh? As much as you care about, anyhow."

"I shall be much more free," she whispered. "Things will be easier. And I've got to marry someone—"

She broke off with another start. There was a sound again behind them. The man heard nothing. The blood in his temples pulsed too loudly, doubtless.

"Well, what is it this time?" he asked sharply.

She was peering into the wood, where the patches of dark shadow and moonlit spaces made odd, irregular patterns in the air. A low branch near them waved slightly in the wind.

"Did you hear?" she asked nervously.

"Wind," he replied, annoyed that her change of mood disturbed his pleasure.

"But something moved—"

"Only a branch. We're quite alone, quite safe, I tell you," and there was a rasping sound in his voice as he said it. "Don't be so imaginative. I can take care of you."

She sprang up. The moonlight caught her figure, revealing its exquisite young curves beneath the smother of costly clothing. Her hair had dropped a little in the struggle. The man eyed her eagerly, making a quick, impatient gesture toward her, then stopped abruptly. He saw terror in her eyes.

"Oh, hark! What's that?" she whispered in a startled voice. She put her finger up. "Oh, let's go back. I don't like this wood. I'm frightened."

"Rubbish," he said, and tried to catch her by the waist.

"It's safer in the house—my room—or yours—" She broke off again. "There it is—don't you hear? It's a footstep!" Her face was whiter than the moon.

"I tell you it's the wind in the branches," he repeated gruffly. "Oh, come on, *do*. We were just getting jolly together. There's nothing to be afraid of. Can't you believe me?" He tried to pull her down upon his knee again with force. His face wore an unpleasant expression that was half leer, half grin.

But the girl stood away from him. She continued to peer nervously about her. She listened intently.

"You give me the creeps!" he exclaimed crossly, clawing at her waist again with passionate eagerness that now betrayed exasperation. His disappointment turned him coarse.

The girl made a quick movement of escape, turning so as to look in every direction. She gave a little scream.

"That *was* a step. Oh, oh, it's close behind us. I heard it. We're being watched!" she cried in terror. She darted toward him, then shrank back. He did not try to touch her this time.

"Moonshine!" he growled. "You've spoilt me—spoilt our chance with your silly nerves."

But she did not hear him apparently. She stood there shivering as with sudden cold.

"There! I saw it again. I'm sure of it. Something went past me through the air."

And the man, still thinking only of his pleasure frustrated, got up heavily, something like anger in his eyes. "All right," he said testily; "if you're going to make a fuss, we'd better go. The house *is* safer, possibly, as you say. You know my room. Come along!" Even that risk he would take. He loved her with his "soul."

They crept stealthily out of the wood, the girl slightly in front of him, casting frightened backward glances. Afraid, guilty, ashamed, with an air as though they had been detected, they stole back toward the garden and the house, and disappeared from view.

And a wind rose suddenly with a rushing sound, poured through the wood as though to cleanse it, swept out the artificial scent and trace of shame, and brought back again the song, the laughter, and the happy revels. It roared across the park, it shook the windows of the house, then sank away as quickly as it came. The trees stood motionless again, guarding their secret in the clean, sweet moonlight that held the world in dream until the dawn stole up, and the sunshine took the earth again with joy.

THE LOST THYRUS
Oliver Onions

From *Widdershins*, 1911

Oliver Onions was best known for his ghost stories, one of which, "The Beckoning Fair One," was called by Algernon Blackwood the best ghost story in English. "The Lost Thyrus" takes us away from the strictly ghostly, into a world where the detritus of myth propels a descent into madness, while we remain very much in doubt about what is true and what is not.

As the young man put his hand to the uppermost of the four brass bell-knobs to the right of the fan lighted door he paused, withdrew the hand again, and then pulled at the lowest knob. The sawing of bell-wire answered him, and he waited for a moment, uncertain whether the bell had rung, before pulling again. Then there came from the basement a single cracked stroke; the head of a maid appeared in the whitewashed area below; and the head was withdrawn as apparently the maid recognized him. Steps were heard along the hall; the door was opened; and the maid stood aside to let him enter, the apron with which she had slipped the latch still crumpled in her greasy hand.

"Sorry, Daisy," the young man apologized, "but I didn't want to bring her down all those stairs. How is she? Has she been out today?"

The maid replied that the person spoken of had been out; and the young man walked along the wide carpeted passage.

It was cumbered like an antique shop, with alabaster busts on pedestals, dusty palms in faience vases, and trophies of spears and shields and assegais. At the foot of the stairs was a rustling portière of strung beads, and beyond it the carpet was continued up the broad, easy flight, secured at each step by a brass rod. Where the stairs made a turn, the fading light of the December afternoon, made still dimmer by a window of decalcomanied glass, shone on a cloudy green aquarium with sallow goldfish, a number of cacti on a shabby console table, and a large and dirty white sheepskin rug. Passing along a short landing, the young man began the ascent of the second flight. This also was carpeted, but with a carpet that had done duty in some dining or bedroom before being cut up into strips of the width of the narrow space between the wall and the handrail. Then, as he still mounted, the young man's feet sounded loud on oilcloth; and when he finally paused and knocked at a door it was on a small landing of naked boards beneath the cold gleam of the skylight above the well of the stairs.

"Come in," a girl's voice called.

The room he entered had a low sagging ceiling on which shone a low glow of firelight, making colder still the patch of eastern sky beyond the roofs and the cowls and hoods of chimneys framed by the square of the single window. The glow on the ceiling was reflected dully in the old dark mirror over the mantelpiece. An open door in the farther corner, hampered with skirts and blouses, allowed a glimpse of the girl's bedroom.

The young man set the paper bag he carried down on the littered round table and advanced to the girl who sat in an old wicker chair before the fire. The girl did not turn her head as he kissed her cheek, and he looked down at something that had muffled the sound of his steps as he had approached her.

"Hallo, that's new, isn't it, Bessie? Where did that come from?" he asked cheerfully.

The middle of the floor was covered with a common jute matting, but on the hearth was a magnificent leopard skin rug.

"Mrs. Hepburn sent it up. There was a draught from under the door. It's much warmer for my feet."

"Very kind of Mrs. Hepburn. Well, how are you feeling today, old girl?"

"Better, thanks, Ed."

"That's the style. You'll be yourself again soon. Daisy says you've been out today?"

"Yes, I went for a walk. But not far; I went to the museum and then sat down. You're early, aren't you?"

He turned away to get a chair, from which he had to move a mass of tissue paper patterns and buckram linings. He brought it to the rug.

"Yes. I stopped last night late to cash up for Vedder, so he's staying tonight. Turn and turn about. Well, tell us all about it, Bess."

Their faces were red in the firelight. Hers had the prettiness that the first glance almost exhausts, the prettiness, amazing in its quantity, that one sees for a moment under the light of the street lamps when shops and offices close for the day. She was short-nosed, pulpy-mouthed, and faunish-eyed, and only the rather remarkable smallness of the head on the splendid thick throat saved her from ordinariness. He, too, might have been seen in his thousands at the close of any day, hurrying home to Catford or Walham Green or

Tufnell Park to tea and an evening with a girl or in a billiard room, or else dining cheaply "up West" preparatory to smoking cigarettes from yellow packets in the upper circle of a music hall. Four inches of white up-and-down collar encased his neck; and as he lifted his trousers at the knee to clear his purple socks, the pair of paper covers showed, that had protected his cuffs during the day at the office. He removed them, crumpled them up and threw them on the fire; and the momentary addition to the light of the upper chamber showed how curd-white was that superb neck of hers and how moody and tired her eyes.

From his face only one would have guessed, and guessed wrongly, that his preferences were for billiard rooms and music halls. His conversation showed them to be otherwise. It was of polytechnic classes that he spoke, and of the course lectures in English literature that had just begun. And, as if somebody had asserted that the pursuit of such studies was not compatible with a certain measure of physical development also, he announced that he was not sure that he should not devote, say, half an evening a week, on Wednesdays, to training in the gymnasium.

"*Mens sana in corpore sano*, Bessie," he said; "a sound mind in a sound body, you know. That's tremendously important, especially when a fellow spends the day in a stuffy office. Yes, I think I shall give it half Wednesdays, from eight-thirty to nine-thirty; sends you home in a glow. But I was going to tell you about the literature class. The second lecture's tonight. The first was splendid, all about the languages of Europe and Asia—what they call the Indo-Germanic languages, you know. Aryans. I can't tell you exactly without my notes, but the Hindus and Persians, I think it was, they crossed the Himalaya Mountains and spread westward somehow, as far as Europe. That was the way it all began. It was splendid, the way the lecturer put it. English is a Germanic language, you know. Then came the Celts. I wish I'd brought my notes. I see you've been reading; let's look—"

A book lay on her knees, its back warped by the heat of the fire. He took it and opened it.

"Ah, Keats! Glad you like Keats, Bessie. We needn't be great readers, but it's important that what we do read should be all right. I don't know him, not *really* know him, that is. But he's quite all right—A-1 in fact. And he's an example of what I've always maintained, that knowledge should be brought within reach of all. It just shows. He was the son of a livery-stable keeper, you know, so what he'd have been if he'd really had chances, been to universities and so on, there's no knowing. But, of course, it's more from the historical standpoint that I'm studying these things. Let's have a look—"

He opened the book where a hairpin between the leaves marked a place. The firelight glowed on the page, and he read, monotonously and inelastically:

"And as I sat, over the light blue hills
There came a noise of revelers; the rills
Into the wide stream came of purple hue—
    'Twas Bacchus and his crew!

The earnest trumpet spake, and the silver thrills
From kissing cymbals made a merry din—
    'Twas Bacchus and his kin!

Like to a moving vintage down they came,
Crowned with green leaves, and faces all aflame;
All madly dancing through the pleasant valley
    To scare thee, Melancholy!"

It was the wondrous passage from *Endymion*, of the
descent of the wild inspired rabble into India. Ed plucked
for a moment at his lower lip, and then, with a "Hm! What's
it all about, Bessie?" continued:

> "Within his car, aloft, young Bacchus stood,
> Trifling his ivy-dart, in dancing mood,
>> With sidelong laughing;
> And little rills of crimson wine imbrued
> His plump white arms and shoulders, enough white
> For Venus' pearly bite;
> And near him rode Silenus on his ass,
> Pelted with flowers as he on did pass,
>> Tipsily quaffing."

"Hm! I see. Mythology. That's made up of tales, and
myths, you know. Like Odin and Thor and those, only those
were Scandinavian mythology. So it would be absurd to take
it too seriously. But I think, in a way, things like that do harm.
You see," he explained, "the more beautiful they are the more
harm they might do. We ought always to show virtue and
vice in their true colors, and if you look at it from that point
of view this is just drunkenness. That's rotten; it destroys
your body and intellect; as I heard a chap say once, it's an
insult to the beasts to call it beastly. I joined the Blue Ribbon
when I was fourteen and I haven't been sorry for it yet. No.
Now there's Vedder; he 'went off on a bend,' as he calls it,
last night, and even he says this morning it wasn't worth it.
But let's read on."

Again he read, with unresilient movement:

> "I saw Osirian Egypt kneel adown
> Before the vine wreath crown!

> I saw parched Abyssinia rouse and sing
> To the silver cymbals' ring!
> I saw the whelming vintage hotly pierce
> Old Tartary the fierce! . . .
> Great Brahma from his mystic heaven groans . . ."

"Hm! He was a Buddhist god, Brahma was; mythology again. As I say, if you take it seriously, it's just glorifying intoxication. —But I say; I can hardly see. Better light the lamp. We'll have tea first, then read. No, you sit still; I'll get it ready; I know where things are—"

He rose, crossed to a little cupboard with a sink in it, filled the kettle at the tap, and brought it to the fire. Then he struck a match and lighted the lamp.

The cheap glass shade was of a foolish corolla shape, clear glass below, shading to pink, and deepening to red at the crimped edge. It gave a false warmth to the spaces of the room above the level of the mantelpiece, and Ed's figure, as he turned the regulator, looked from the waist upwards as if he stood within that portion of a spectrum screen that deepens to the band of red. The bright concentric circles that spread in rings of red on the ceiling were more dimly reduplicated in the old mirror over the mantelpiece; and the wintry eastern light beyond the chimney hoods seemed suddenly almost to die out.

Bessie, her white neck below the level of the lampshade, had taken up the book again; but she was not reading. She was looking over it at the upper part of the grate. Presently she spoke.

"I was looking at some of those things this afternoon, at the museum."

He was clearing from the table more buckram linings and

patterns of paper, numbers of *Myra's Journal* and *The Delineator*. Already on his way to the cupboard he had put aside a red-bodiced dressmaker's "shape" of wood and wire.

"What things?" he asked.

"Those you were reading about. Greek, aren't they?"

"Oh, the Greek room! . . . But those people, Bacchus and those, weren't people in the ordinary sense. Gods and goddesses most of 'em; Bacchus was a god. That's what mythology means. I wish sometimes our course took in Greek literature, but it's a dead language after all. German's more good in modern life. It would be nice to know everything, but one has to select, you know. Hallo, I clean forgot; I brought you some grapes, Bessie; here they are, in this bag; we'll have some after tea, what?"

"But," she said again after a pause, still looking at the grate, "they had their priests and priestesses, and followers and people, hadn't they? It was their things I was looking at—combs and brooches and hairpins, and things to cut their nails with. They're all in a glass case there. And they had safety pins, exactly like ours."

"Oh, they were a civilized people," said Ed cheerfully. "It all gives you an idea. I only hope you didn't tire yourself out. You'll soon be all right, or course, but you have to be careful yet. We'll have a clean tablecloth, shall we?"

She had been seriously ill; her life had been despaired of; and somehow the young polytechnic student seemed anxious to assure her that she was now all right again, or soon would be. They were to be married "as soon as things brightened up a bit," and he was very much in love with her. He watched her head and neck as he continued to lay the table, and then, as he crossed once more to the cupboard, he put his hand lightly in passing on her hair.

She gave so quick a start that he too started. She must have been very deep in her reverie to have been so taken by surprise.

"I say, Bessie, don't jump like that!" he cried with involuntary quickness. Indeed, had his hand been red hot, or ice cold, or taloned, she could not have turned a more startled, even frightened, face to him.

"It was your touching me," she muttered, resuming her gaze into the grate.

He stood looking anxiously down on her. It would have been better not to discuss her state, and he knew it; but in his anxiety he forgot it.

"That jumpiness is the effect of your illness; you know I shall be glad when it's all over. It's made you so odd."

She was not pleased that he should speak of her "oddness." For that matter, she, too, found him "odd"—at any rate, found it difficult to realize that he was as he always had been. He had begun to irritate her a little. His clubfooted reading of the verses had irritated her, and she had tried hard to hide from him that his cocksure opinions and the tone in which they were pronounced jarred on her. It was not that she was "better" than he, "knew" any more than he did, didn't (she supposed) love him still the same; these moods, that dated from her illness, had nothing to do with those things; she reproached herself sometimes that she was the subject to such doldrums.

"It's all right, Ed, but please don't touch me just now," she said.

He was in the act of leaning over her chair, but he saw her shrink, and refrained.

"Poor old girl!" he said sympathetically. "What's the matter?"

"I don't know. It's awfully stupid of me to be like this, but I can't help it. I shall be better soon if you leave me alone."

"Nothing's happened, has it?"

"Only those silly dreams I told you about."

"Bother the dreams!" muttered the polytechnic student.

During her illness she had had dreams, and had come to herself at intervals to find Ed or the doctor, Mrs. Hepburn or her aunt, bending over her. These kind, solicitous faces had been no more than a glimpse, and then she had gone off into the dreams again. The curious thing had been that the dreams had seemed to be her vivid waking life, and the other things—the anxious faces, the details of her dingy bedroom, the thermometer under her tongue—had been the dream. And, though she had come back to actuality, the dreams had never quite vanished. She could remember no more of them than that they had seemed to hold a high singing and jocundity, issuing from some region of haze and golden light; and they seemed to hover, ever on the point of being recaptured, yet ever eluding all her mental efforts. She was living now between reality and a vision.

She had fewer words than sensations, and it was a little pitiful to hear her vainly striving to make clear what she meant.

"It's so queer," she said. "It's like being on the edge of something—a sort of tiptoe—I can't describe it. Sometimes I could almost touch it with my hand, and then it goes away, but never *quite* away. It's like something just past the corner of my eye, over my shoulder, and I sit very still sometimes, trying to take it off its guard. But the moment I move my head it moves too—like this—"

Again he gave a quick start at the suddenness of her action. Very stealthily her faunish eyes had stolen sideways, and then she had swiftly turned her head.

"Here, I say, don't, Bessie!" he cried nervously. "You look awfully uncanny when you do that! You're brooding," he continued, "that's what you're doing, brooding. You're getting in a low state. You want bucking up. I don't think I shall go up to the polytechnic tonight; I shall stay and cheer you up. You know, I really don't think you're making an effort, darling."

His last words seemed to strike her. They seemed to fit in with something of which she too was conscious. "Not making an effort..." She wondered how he knew that. She felt in some vague way that it was important that she *should* make an effort.

For, while her dream ever evaded her, and yet never ceased to call her with such a voice as he who reads on a magic page of the calling of elves hears stilly in his brain, yet somehow behind the seduction was another and a sterner voice. There was warning as well as fascination. Beyond that edge at which she strained on tiptoe, mingled with the jocund calls to Hasten, Hasten, were deeper calls that bade her Beware. They puzzled her. Beware of what? Of what danger? And to whom?...

"How do you mean, I'm not making an effort, Ed?" she asked slowly, again looking into the fire, where the kettle now made a gnat-like singing.

"Why, an effort to get all right again. To be as you used to be—as, of course, you will be soon."

"As I *used* to be?" The words came with a little check in her breathing.

"Yes, before all this. To be yourself, you know."

"Myself?"

"All jolly, and without these jerks and jumps. I wish you could get away. A fortnight by the sea would do you all the good in the world."

97

She knew not what it was in the words "the sea" that caused her suddenly to breathe more deeply. The sea!… It was as if, by the mere uttering of them, he had touched some secret spring, brought to fulfillment some spell. What had he meant by speaking of the sea?… A fortnight before, had somebody spoken to her of the sea it would have been the sea of Margate, of Brighton, of Southend, that, supplying the image that a word calls up as if by conjuration, she would have seen before her; and what other she could supply, could she *possibly* supply, now?… Yet she did, or almost did, supply one. What new experience had she had, or what old, old one had been released in her? With that confused, joyous dinning just beyond the range of physical hearing there had suddenly mingled a new illusion of sound—a vague, vast pash and rustle, silky and harsh both at once, its tireless voice holding meanings of stillness and solitude compared with which the silence that is mere absence of sound was vacancy. It was part of her dream, invisible, intangible, inaudible, yet there. As if he had been an enchanter, it had come into being at the word upon his lips. Had he other such words? Had he the Master Word that—(ah, she knew what the Master Word would do!)—would make the Vision the Reality and the Reality the Vision? Deep within her she felt something—her soul, herself, she knew not what—thrill and turn over and settle again.…

"The sea," she repeated in a low voice.

"Yes, that's what you want to set you up—rather! Do you remember that fortnight at Littlehampton, you and me and your aunt? Jolly that was! I like Littlehampton. It isn't flash like Brighton, and Margate's always so beastly crowded. And do you remember that afternoon by the windmill? I did love you that afternoon, Bessie!"

He continued to talk, but she was not listening. She was wondering why the words "the sea" were somehow part of it all—the pins and brooches of the museum, the book on her knees, the dream. She remembered a game of hide-and-seek she had played as a child, in which cries of "Warm, warm, warmer!" had announced the approach to the hidden object. Oh, she was getting warm—positively hot....

He had ceased to talk, and was watching her. Perhaps it was the thought of how he had loved her that afternoon by the windmill that had brought him close to her chair again. She was aware of his nearness, and closed her eyes for a moment as if she dreaded something. Then she said quickly, "Is tea nearly ready, Ed?" and, as he turned to the table, took up the book again.

She felt that even to touch that book brought her "warmer." It fell open at a page. She did not hear the clatter Ed made at the table, nor yet the babble his words had evoked, of the pierrots and banjos and minstrels of Margate and Littlehampton. It was to hear a gladder, wilder tumult that she sat once so still, so achingly listening....

"The earnest trumpet spake, and silver thrills
From kissing cymbals made a merry din—"

The words seemed to move on the page. In her eyes another light than the firelight seemed to play. Her breast rose, and in her thick white throat a little inarticulate sound twanged.

"Eh? Did you speak, Bessie?" Ed asked, stopping in his buttering of bread.

"Eh?... No."

In answering, her head had turned for a moment, and she had seen him. Suddenly it struck her with force: a shaving of a man he was! Desk-chested, weak-necked, conscious of

his little "important" lip and chin—yes, he needed a polytechnic gymnastic course! Then she remarked how once, at
Margate, she had seen him in the distance, as in a hired baggy
bathing-dress he had bathed from a machine, in muddy
water, one of a hundred others, all rather cold, flinging a polo
ball about and shouting stridently. "A sound mind in a sound
body!"... He was rather vain in his neat shoes, too, and doubtless stunted his feet; and she had seen the little spot on his
neck caused by the chafing of his collar stud.... No, she did
not want him to touch her, just now at any rate. His touch
would be too like a betrayal of another touch ... somewhere,
sometime, somehow ... in that tantalizing dream that refused
to allow itself either to be fully remembered or quite forgotten. What *was* that dream? *What* was it?...

She continued to gaze into the fire.

Of a sudden she sprang to her feet with a choked cry of
almost animal fury. The fool *had* touched her. Carried away
doubtless by the memory of that afternoon by the windmill,
he had, in passing once more to the kettle, crept softly behind
her and put a swift burning kiss on the side of her neck.

Then he had retreated before her, stumbling against the
table and causing the cups and saucers to jingle.

The basket chair tilted up, but righted itself again.

"I told you—I told you—" she choked, her stockish figure
shaking with rage, "I told you—you—"

He put up his elbow as if to ward off a blow.

"You touch me—*you!*—*you!*" the words broke from her.

He had put himself farther around the table. He stammered.

"Here—dash it all, Bessie—what *is* the matter?"

"*You* touch me!"

"All right," he said sullenly. "I won't touch you again—

no fear. I didn't know you were such a firebrand. All right, drop it now. I won't again. Good Lord!"

Slowly the white fist she had drawn back sank to her side again.

"All right now," he continued to grumble resentfully. "You needn't take on so. It's said—I won't touch you again." Then, as if he remembered that after all she was ill and must be humored, he began, while her bosom still rose and fell rapidly, to talk with an assumption that nothing much had happened. "Come, sit down again, Bessie. The tea's in the pot and I'll have it ready in a couple of jiffs. What a ridiculous little girl you are, to take on like that!... And I say, listen! That's a muffin bell and a grand fire for toast! You sit down while I run out and get 'em. Give me your key, so I can let myself in again—"

He took her key from her bag, caught up his hat, and hastened out.

But she did not sit down again. She was no calmer for his quick disappearance. In that moment when he had recoiled from her she had had the expression of some handsome and angered snake, its hood puffed, ready to strike. She stood dazed; one would have supposed that the ill-advised kiss of his had indeed been the Master Word she sought, the Word she felt approaching, the Word to which the objects of the museum, the book, that rustle of a sea she had never seen, had been but the ever "warming" stages. Some merest trifle stood between her and those elfin cries, between her and that thin golden mist in which faintly seen shapes seemed to move—shapes almost of tossed arms, waving, brandishing objects strangely all but familiar. That roaring of the sea was *not* the rushing of her own blood in her ears, that rosy flush *not* the artificial glow of the cheap red lampshade. The shapes were almost as plain as if she saw them in some clear but black mirror, the sounds almost as audible as if she heard them through some not very thick muffling. . . .

"Quick—the book," she muttered.

But even as she stretched out her hand for it, again came that solemn sound of warning. As if something sought to stay it, she had deliberately to thrust her hand forward. Again the high dinning calls of "Hasten! Hasten!" were mingled with that deeper "Beware!" She knew in her soul that, once over that terrible edge, the Dream would become the Reality and the Reality the Dream. She knew nothing of the fluidity of the thing called Personality—not a thing at all, but a state, a balance, a relation, a resultant of forces so delicately in equilibrium that a touch, and—*pff!*—the horror of Formlessness rushed over all.

As she hesitated a new light appeared in the chamber. Within the frame of the small square window, beyond the ragged line of the chimney cowls, an edge of orange brightness showed. She leaned forward. It was the full moon, rusty and bloated and flattened by the earth-mist.

The next moment her hand had clutched at the book.

"Whence came ye, merry damsels! Whence came ye
So many, and so many, and such glee?
Why have ye left your bowers desolate,
       Your lutes, and gentler fate?
'We follow Bacchus, Bacchus on the wing
       A-conquering!
Bacchus, young Bacchus! Good or ill betide
We dance before him through kingdoms wide!
Come hither, Lady fair, and joinèd be
       To our wild minstrelsy!"

There was an instant in which darkness seemed to blot out all else; then it rolled aside, and in a blaze of brightness was gone. It was gone, and she stood face to face with her Dream, that for two thousand years had slumbered in the blood of her and her line. She stood, with mouth agape and eyes that hailed, her thick throat full of suppressed clamor. The other was the Dream now, and *these!* ... they came down, mad and noisy and bright—Mænades, Thyades, satyrs, fauns—naked, in hides of beasts, ungirdled, disheveled, wreathed and garlanded, dancing, singing, shouting. The thudding of their hooves shook the ground, and the clash of their timbrels and the rustling of their thyrsi filled the air. They brandished frontal bones, the dismembered quarters of kids and goats; they struck the bronze cantharus, they tossed the silver obba aloft. Down a cleft of rocks and wood they came, trooping to a wide seashore with the red of the sunset behind them. She saw the evening light on the sleek and dappled hides, the gilded ivory and rich brown of their legs and shoulders, the white of inner arms held up on high, their wide red mouths, the quivering of the twin flesh-gouts on the necks of the leaping fauns. And, shutting out the glimpse of sky at the head of the deep ravine, the god himself descended, with his car full of drunken girls who slept with the serpents coiled about them.

Shouting and moaning and frenzied, leaping upon one another with libidinous laughter and beating one another with the half-stripped thyrsi, they poured down to the yellow sands and the anemonied pools of the shore. They raced to the water, that gleamed pale as nacre in the deepening twilight in the eye of the evening star. They ran along its edge over the images in the wet sands, calling their lost companion.

"Hasten, hasten!" they cried; and one of them, a young man with a torso noble as the dawn and shoulder lines strong as those of the eternal hills, ran here and there calling her name.

"Louder, louder!" she called back in an ecstasy.

Something dropped and tinkled against the fender. It was one of her hairpins. One side of her hair was in a loose tumble; she threw up the small head on the superb thick neck.

"Louder!—I cannot hear! Once more—"

The throwing up of her head that had brought down the rest of her hair had given her a glimpse of herself in the glass over the mantelpiece. For the last time that formidable "Beware!" sounded like thunder in her ears; the next moment she had snapped with her fingers the ribbon that was cutting into her throbbing throat. He with the torso and shoulders was seeking her … how should he know her in that dreary garret, in those joyless habiliments? He would as soon know his Own in that crimson-bodiced, wire-framed dummy by the window yonder! …

Her fingers clutched at the tawdry mercerised silk of her blouse. There was a rip, and her arms and throat were free. She panted as she tugged at something that gave with a short "click-click," as of steel fastenings; something fell against the fender.... These also.... She tore at them, and kicked them as they lay about her feet as leaves lie about the trunk of a tree in autumn....

"*Ah!*"

And as she stood there, as if within the screen of a spectrum that deepened to the band of red, her eyes fell on the leopard skin at her feet. She caught it up, and in doing so saw purple grapes—purple grapes that issued from the mouth of a paper bag on the table. With the dappled pelt about her she sprang forward. The juice spurted through them into the mass of her loosened hair. Down her body there was a spill of seeds and pulp. She cried hoarsely aloud.

"Once more—oh, answer me! Tell me my name!"

Ed's steps were heard on the oilclothed portion of the staircase.

"My name—oh, my name!" she cried in an agony of suspense.... "Oh, they will not wait for me! They have lighted the torches—they run up and down the shore with torches—oh, cannot you see me?..."

Suddenly she dashed to the chair on which the litter of linings and tissue paper lay. She caught up a double handful and crammed them on the fire. They caught and flared. There was a call upon the stairs, and the sound of somebody mounting in haste.

"Once—once only—my name!"

The soul of the Bacchante rioted, struggled to escape from her eyes. Then as the door was flung open, she heard, and gave a terrifying shout of recognition.

"I hear—I almost hear—but once more.... IO! *Io, Io, Io!*"

Ed, in the doorway, stood for one moment agape; the next, ignorant of the full purport of his own words—ignorant that though man may come westward he may yet bring his worship with him—ignorant that to make the Dream the Reality and the Reality the Dream is Heaven's dreadfullest favor—and ignorant that, that Edge once crossed, there is no return to sanity and sweetness and light that are only seen clearly in the moment when they are lost forever—he had dashed down the stairs crying in a voice hoarse and high terror:

"She's mad! She's mad!"

"I AM DIONYSUS…"

Euripides, from *The Bacchae*

Adapted by Stefan Rudnicki

First performed at the Greek Great Dionysia Festival,
405 BCE

Representing variously the powers of sexual abandon, intoxication, and the subconscious itself, Dionysus or Bacchus, or the lesser persona, Pan, have figured prominently in the dreams and fears of Western civilization … civilized, some might say, by the denial of those very qualities. One of the earliest manifestations is in Euripides' tragedy, *The Bacchae*, in which Dionysus acts like a spoiled child who does not get the attention he thinks he deserves. Having tricked Queen Agave and her team of wild women into killing and dismembering her son Pentheus, he now proclaims doom on her and her father, King Kadmus. In this, one of the earliest of horror/fantasy stories, Euripides personifies all fears—including terror of the unexpected—in one being, Dionysus, and lays all our nightmares at his gate.

Dionysus appears in his god form on the roof of the palace.

DIONYSUS
I am Dionysus, the god, son of Zeus,

Come back to Thebes where I was born,
And where I was also thrown in prison,
Insulted and blasphemed. Hear now the end.
To salvage Thebes from cursed pollution,
Queen Agave and her sisters will leave Thebes,
Never to return.
These are the words of Dionysus, god,
Not human words.
Had you chosen wisdom,
Had you not descended into madness,
As you did, the god, the son of Zeus,
I, Dionysus, would now be your friend,
Fighting at your side forever,
Leading you at peace.

KADMUS
Dionysus, have mercy on us. We admit we wronged you.

DIONYSUS
Too late. When there was time, you did not know me.

AGAVE
We know you now. You are pure Vengeance.

DIONYSUS
I am a god. I was blasphemed. There can be no forgiveness.

AGAVE
The gods should be better than men, and show compassion.

DIONYSUS
The gods *are* better, and beyond the scope
Of human understanding. Zeus, my father,
Made the laws of balance and revenge
At the beginning of time. There can be no forgiveness.

AGAVE
to Kadmus
Father! The word has been spoken. We are exiled.

DIONYSUS
What are you waiting for? Your fate is set.

AGAVE
Farewell, my land, my home,
This house where long ago I came a bride.

KADMUS
Mourn for each other and for our dead.

AGAVE
Lord Dionysus dooms us all.

DIONYSUS
from above
Was I honored? No!
I was blasphemed.

CHORUS
The gods have many faces.
They show themselves to us in many ways.
What seems certain is uncertain.
What we expect can never happen.
Only the unforeseen, the unexpected,
Is the unforgiving and eternal province of the gods.
Today, we have been shown the truth.

Part Two

OTHER MYTHS

"A NOISELESS PATIENT SPIDER"

An excerpt from *Whispers of Heavenly Death*

Walt Whitman

From *Leaves of Grass,* 1900

A noiseless patient spider,
I mark'd where on a little promontory it stood isolated,
Mark'd how to explore the vacant surrounding,
It launch'd forth filament, filament, filament, out of itself,
Ever unreeling them, ever tirelessly speeding them.

And you, O my soul where you stand,
Surrounded, detached, in measureless oceans of space,
Ceaselessly musing, venturing, throwing, seeking the
  spheres to connect them,
Till the bridge you will need be form'd, till the ductile
  anchor hold,
Till the gossamer thread you fling catch somewhere,
  O my soul.

What if the powers, gods, or creatures that surround our pitifully small known existence don't conform to traditional mythology? What if there are "others" for which we have no context, and of which we can have no possible understanding? This section provides a variety of solutions for how to deal with the nameless terrors, the hidden powers, the gods of other universes.

MYSTERY TRAIN

For Bruce Sterling

Lewis Shiner

Written in 1983, featured in the author's first story collection,
Love in Vain, 2001

One way to fill the mythic vacuum is to create our own immediate heroes and gods, elevating our pop icons to even greater heights. Elvis, Sinatra, Janis—already elevated by the power of music—were perhaps moved by forces we can only guess at. In "Mystery Train," Lewis Shiner takes real people in a real time, and then jumbles past and future on a television screen until we feel that there are things indeed better not known.

As he climbed the stairs, Elvis popped the cap off the pill bottle and shook a couple more Dexedrines into his palm. They looked like pink candy hearts, lying there. He tossed them into the back of his throat and swallowed them dry.

"Hey, Elvis, man, are you sure you want to keep taking those things?" Charlie was half a flight behind, drunk and out of breath. "I mean, you been flying on that shit all weekend."

"I can handle it, man. Don't sweat it." Actually the last round of pills hadn't affected him at all, and now his muscles burned and his head felt like a bowling ball. He collapsed in an armchair in the third floor bedroom, as far as possible from the noise of the reporters and the kids and the girls who stood outside the house. "In three weeks we're out of here, man. Out of Germany, out of the Army, out of these goddamn uniforms." He untied his shoes and kicked them off.

"Amen, brother."

"Charlie, turn on the goddamn TV, will you?"

"Come on, man, that thing's got a remote control, and I ain't it."

"Okay, okay." Elvis lunged for the remote control box and switched on the brand-new RCA color console. It was the best money could buy, the height of American technology, even if Germany didn't have any color transmissions to pick up with it.

Charlie had collapsed across the bed. "Hey, Elvis. When you get home, man, you ought to get yourself three different TVs. I mean, you're the king, right? That way, not only can you fuck more girls than anybody and make more money than anybody and take more pills than anybody, you can watch more TV than anybody, too. You can have a different goddamn TV for every channel. One for ABC...." He yawned. "One for NBC...." He was asleep.

"Charlie?" Elvis said. "Charlie, you lightweight." He looked around the edge of the chair and saw Charlie's feet hanging off the end of the bed, heel up and perfectly still.

To hell with it, Elvis thought, flipping through the channels. Let him sleep. They'd had a rough weekend, driving into Frankfurt in the BMW and picking up some girls, skating on the icy roads all across the north end of Germany, hitting the booze and pills. In the old days it had annoyed Elvis mightily that his body couldn't tolerate alcohol, but ever since one of his sergeants had given him his first Dexedrine he hadn't missed booze at all. Charlie still liked the bottle, but for Elvis there was nothing like that rush of power he got from the pills.

Well, there was one thing, of course, and that was being on stage. It was not quite two years now since he'd been inducted—since Monday, March 24, 1958, and he'd been counting the days. The Colonel had said no USO shows, no nothing until he was out. Nobody got Elvis for free.

The Colonel had come to take the place of his mother, who had died while Elvis was still in basic, and his father, who had betrayed Gladys's memory by seeing other women. There was no one else that Elvis could respect, that he could look to for advice. If the Colonel said no shows then that was it.

Something flashed on the TV screen. Elvis backed through the dead channels to find it again, ending up with a screen full of electronic snow. He got up and played with the fine tuning ring to see if he could sharpen it any.

Memories of his early years haunted him. Those had been the best times, hitting the small towns with just Scotty and Bill, the equipment strapped to the top of Scotty's brand-new, red-and-white '56 Chevy. Warming the audience up with something slow, like "Old Shep," then laying them out, ripping the joint with "Good Rockin' Tonight." Getting out of control, his legs shaking like he had epilepsy, forgetting to play the guitar, his long hair sticking out in front like the bill of a cap, taking that mike stand all the way to the floor and making love to it, shaking and sweating and feeling the force and power of the music hit those kids in the guts like cannon fire.

He gave up on the TV picture and paced the room, feeling the first pricklings of the drug. His eyelids had started to vibrate and he could feel each of the individual hairs on his arms.

When he sat down again there was something on the screen.

It looked like a parade, with crowds on both sides of the street and a line of cars approaching. They were black limousines, convertibles, with people waving from the back seats. Elvis thought he recognized one of the faces, a Senator from up north, the one everybody said was going to run for President.

He tried the sound. It was in German and he couldn't make any sense of it. The only German words he'd learned had been in bed, and they weren't the kind that would show up on television.

The amphetamine hit him just as the senator's head blew apart.

Elvis watched the chunks of brain and blood fly through the air in slow motion. For a second he couldn't believe what he was seeing, then he jumped up and grabbed Charlie by the shoulder.

"Charlie, wake up! C'mon man, this is serious!" Charlie rolled onto his back, eyes firmly shut, a soft snore buzzing in his throat. No amount of shaking could wake him up.

On the television, men in dark suits swarmed over the car as it picked up speed and disappeared down the road. The piece of film ran out, hanging in the projector for a moment, then the screen turned white.

He went back to the chair and stood with his hands resting on its high, curved back. Had he really seen what he thought he saw? Or was it just the drugs? He dug his fingers into the dingy gray-green fabric of the chair, the same fabric he'd seen by the mile all through Europe. He was tired of old things: old chairs, old wood-floored houses, Frau Gross, the old woman who lived with them, the old buildings, and cobbled streets of Bad Nauheim.

America, he thought, here I come. Clean your glass and polish your chrome and wax your linoleum tile.

The TV flickered and showed a hotel room with an unmade bed and clothes all around. On the nightstand was an overflowing ashtray and an empty bottle. Elvis recognized the Southern Comfort label even in the grainy picture. A woman sat on the floor with her back against the bed. She had ratty hair and a flabby, pinched sort of face. The nipples of her small breasts showed through her T-shirt, which looked like somebody had spilled paint and bleach all over it.

Elvis thought she must be some kind of down-and-out hooker. He was a little disgusted by the sight of her. Still he couldn't look away as she brought a loaded hypodermic up to her arm and found a vein.

Static shot across the screen and the image broke up. Diagonal lines scrolled past a field of fuzzy gray. Elvis felt the Dexedrine bounce his heart against the conga drum of his chest. He sat down to steady himself, his finger rattling lightly against the arm of the chair.

"Man," Elvis said to the room, "I am really fucked up."

A new voice came out of the TV. It must have originally belonged to some German girl, breathy and sexual, but bad recording had turned it into a mechanical whisper. Another room took shape, another rumpled bed, this one with a black man lying on it, long frizzy hair pressed against the pillow, a trickle of vomit running out of his mouth. He bucked twice, his long, muscular fingers clawing at the air, and lay still.

Elvis pushed the heels of his hands into his burning eyes. It's the drugs, he thought. The drugs and not sleeping and knowing I'm going home in a couple of weeks....

He wandered into the hall, one hand on the crumbling plaster wall to steady himself. He tried the handle on the room next to his but the door refused to open.

"Red? Hey, Red, get your ass up and answer this door." He slapped the wood a couple of times and then gave up, afraid to deal with Frau Gross when he was so far gone. He went into the bathroom instead and splashed cold water on his face, letting it soak the collar of his shirt. He wouldn't miss this screwy European plumbing, either.

"I feel so good," he sang to himself, "I'm living in the USA...." He looked like shit. With his green fatigues and sallow skin he looked like a fucking Christmas tree, with two ornaments where his eyes were supposed to be.

He went back to the bedroom and sat down again. He needed sleep. He'd find something, like "Bonanza" in German, and maybe he could doze off in the chair.

As he reached for the remote, another film started. It was scratched and grainy and not quite in focus. Some fat guy in a white suit was hanging on to a mike stand and mumbling. It was impossible to understand what he said, especially with the nasal German narration that ran on top. Elvis made out a lot of "you knows" and "well, wells."

The camera moved in and Elvis went cold. Despite his age and his blubber and his long, girlish hair, the guy was trying to do an Elvis imitation. A band started up in the background and the fat man began to sing.

The Colonel had warned him this might happen. You don't drop out for two years and not expect somebody to try and cut you. Bobby Darin with all his finger-popping and that simpering Ricky Nelson had been bad enough, but this was really the end. Elvis had never heard the song that the fat guy was trying to sing. He was obviously being carried by the size of the orchestra behind him. Pathetic, Elvis thought. A joke. The fat guy curled his lip, threw a couple of karate punches, and let one leg begin to shake.

Dear God, Elvis thought.

It wasn't possible.

Elvis lurched out of the chair and yanked Charlie out of bed by the ankles. "Wha...?" Charlie moaned.

"Get up. Get up and look at this shit."

Charlie struggled to a sitting position and scrubbed his eyes with his hands. "I don't see nothing."

"On the TV, man. You got eyes in your head?"

"There's nothing there, man. Nothing."

Elvis turned, saw snowy interference blocking out the signal again. "Get a chair," Elvis said.

"Aw, man, I'm really whacked...."

"Get the goddamn chair."

Elvis sat back in front of the TV, his heels pounding jump time against the hardwood floor. He heard Charlie dragging a chair up the stairs as the screen cleared and a caption flashed below the singer's face.

Rapid City, South Dakota, it said.

June, 1977.

Elvis didn't know he was on his feet, didn't know he had the service automatic in his hand until his finger went tight on the trigger.

Huge white letters filled the screen.

ELVIS, they said.

He fired. The roar of the gun seemed to make the entire building jump. The picture tube blew in with a sharp crack and a shower of glass. Sparks hissed out on the floor and a single breath of sour smoke wafted out of the ruined set.

Elvis felt the room buzz with hostile forces. He had to get out. Charlie stood in the doorway, staring open-mouthed at the ruins of the set as Elvis shoved past him, letting the gun drop from his nerveless fingers and clatter across the floor. It wasn't until he was downstairs and the cold air hit him that he realized he'd left his shoes and coat inside. The sidewalk was slick with ice and a mixture of sleet and rain fell as he stood there, eyes jerking back and forth, fingers twitching, legs tensed to run and go on running.

It had to be a mistake, he thought. Something from a burlesque show over in Frankfurt, maybe. Somebody had just screwed up the titles, gotten the date wrong.

Yeah, and the wrong name too.

The silence closed in on him. For the first time since they'd moved into the house on Goethestrasse there weren't any people on the street. In the distance, whining high and faint like a mosquito's wings, he heard a motorcycle approaching. It was the only sound in the night.

He started to feel the cold. Still it wasn't bad enough to make him go back inside, to face the empty, staring socket of the TV set. He shivered, lifted one foot off the icy pavement.

A light winked at him from the end of the street. The motorcycle, coming toward him, rattled like machine gun fire and echoed off the wet streets and flat brick walls. It was moving too fast for the icy roads and the driver seemed barely in control. He slid in and out of the streetlamps' circles of light, shadowy in leather and denim.

Something like a premonition made Elvis start to turn and run back inside. The cold had numbed him and he couldn't seem to get the message through to his legs.

The bike skidded to a stop in front of the house and its engine died.

For a second Elvis and the rider stared at each other in the silent moonlight. The rider had no helmet or goggles, just a pair of round, tortoise-shell glasses. Frost and bits of ice had clumped in his hair and the creases of his jacket. A cigarette hung out of the corner of his mouth, and Elvis was sure that if he could have seen the man's face he would have recognized him.

But the man's face was gone. Scars flowed and branched like rivers across the dead white skin of his cheeks. He had no eyebrows, and patches of hair were missing from his temples and forehead. One eye was permanently half-closed and the other was low enough to throw the ruined face off balance. The nose was little more than a flat place and the mouth smiled on one side and frowned on the other.

"Hey," the rider said.

"What?" Elvis was startled by the man's American accent.

"Hey, man. What happened to your shoes?"

The voice was maddeningly familiar. "Who are you?"

"You look shook, man." The scarred mouth stretched in what might have been a grin. "Like, 'All Shook Up,' right?"

"Dean," Elvis said, stunned. "Jimmy Dean, the actor."

The rider shrugged.

"You're dead," Elvis said. "I saw pictures in the paper. That car was torn to pieces, man."

Dean, if that was truly who it was, touched the underside of his mutilated eye and rubbed it softly, as if remembering pain that Elvis could not even imagine.

"What are you doing here?"

Dean shrugged again. "They just, like, wanted me to come by and check up on you. It looks like you already got the message." He rose up on the bike, about to kick the starter, and Elvis moved toward him.

"Wait! Who's 'they'? What do you know about...." He stopped himself. Dean couldn't possibly know anything about what Elvis had seen on TV.

"Hey, be cool, man. If they wanted you to know who they were, then they would tell you, dig? I mean, they didn't even tell me shit, you know?" Dean looked him over. "But I can take a guess, man. I can take a real good guess what they want with you. I seen you on TV, the way you shake your legs and all that. The way you dress like a spade and sing all those raunchy songs. You scare people, man. People think you want to fuck all their daughters and turn their sons into hoods. They don't like that, man."

"I never tried to scare nobody," Elvis said.

Dean giggled. Coming out of that scarred mouth, it was terrifying. "Yeah, right. That's what I used to say."

"What do you mean? Are you threatening me?"

"No threats, man. You're the King. You know? You're the fucking King of America. King of all the cheeseburgers and pink Cadillacs and prescription drugs and handguns in the greatest country in the world. Shit, you are America. They don't have to threaten you. They don't have to hurt you. Just a little nudge here and a little nudge there, and you'll fall right in line."

A door slammed and Charlie came staggering down the sidewalk. "Elvis? What the fuck, man?"

Dean looked like he wanted to say something else, then changed his mind. He started the bike, hunched his shoulders, and sped away.

"Jesus Christ," Charlie said. "You know who that was?"

"It was nobody," Elvis said. He put his hand in the middle

of Charlie's chest and shoved him back toward the house. "Understand? It was nobody."

"There's going to be a new Elvis, brand new. I don't think he will go back to sideburns or ducktails. He's twenty-five now, and he has genuine adult appeal. I think he's going to surprise everyone...."

—Colonel Tom Parker, on Elvis' return from Germany

During rehearsals Elvis kept the windows of his hotel room covered with aluminum foil. It kept out the light and there was something comforting about having it there. It might even keep his TV set from picking up weird, lying broadcasts that would mess with his head. Just in case, he kept a loaded .45 on the bedside table, ready to blow the whole thing away. When forced to go out of the hotel, he kept his bodyguards with him at all times, the ones the papers had started to call his "Memphis Mafia."

He stayed inside as much as he could. The Florida air was hot and dead, seemed to pull the life right out of him. It had been the same in California and Las Vegas, everywhere he'd been since he came home from Germany. Everything was dry and hot and still. He started to believe it would be dry and hot and still forever.

As they taped the opening of the show he fought, without much success, to control his unease. They had him in his Army uniform again, walking out onstage to shake hands with Sinatra and his entire Rat Pack, all of them in tuxedos, mugging the camera, slapping each other on the back.

Over and over he caught himself thinking: What am I doing here?

He worked his way through the crowd, the faces blurring together into a single entity with Bishop's mocking smile, Davis' processed hair and hideous rings, Lawford's limp handshake and Martin's whiskey breath. He had to learn to be comfortable with them. The Colonel had told him how it was going to be, and it was far too late to argue with the Colonel.

It happened while they were taping his duet with Sinatra, Sinatra who had called rock and roll "phony" and the singers "goons" just a couple of years before. Now they were trading verses, Elvis singing "Witchcraft" and Sinatra doing "Love Me Tender."

The scream came from somewhere toward the front of the audience. "That's not him!" It was a girl's voice, and it sounded at least as frightened as it was angry. The stage lights were blinding and Elvis couldn't see her face. "That's not Elvis!" she screamed. "What did you do with him?" The orchestra stopped and the girl's voice carried on unaccompanied. "Where is he? Where's Elvis?"

Elvis saw Sinatra make a gesture toward the wings. A moment later there were muffled voices from the audience and then a vast empty silence.

"Don't worry," Sinatra said. "You're one of us now. We'll take good care of you."

"Yes, sir." Elvis nodded and closed his eyes. "Yes, sir," he said.

CONTINUED ON NEXT ROCK

R.A. Lafferty

First appeared in *Orbit* 7, 1970

And what about archeology? R.A. Lafferty's vastly complex puzzle of human and inhuman relationships, "Continued on Next Rock," suggests that when we meddle with hidden strata of pre-history, we may be invoking powers that can interact with us in terrifying and unpredictable ways.

Up in the Big Lime country there is an up-thrust, a chimney rock that is half fallen against a newer hill. It is formed of what is sometimes called Dawson sandstone and is interlaced with tough shell. It was formed during the glacial and recent ages in the bottom lands of Crow Creek and Green River when these streams (at least five times) were mighty rivers.

The chimney rock is only a little older than mankind, only a little younger than grass. Its formation had been up-thrust and then eroded away again, all but such harder parts as itself and other chimneys and blocks.

A party of five persons came to this place where the chimney rock had fallen against a still newer hill. The people of the party did not care about the deep limestone below; they were not geologists. They *did* care about the newer hill (it was manmade) and they did care a little about the rock chimney; they were archaeologists.

Here was time heaped up, bulging out in casing and accumulation, and not in line sequence. And here also was striated and banded time, grown tall, and then shattered and broken.

The five party members came to the site early in the afternoon, bringing the working trailer down a dry creek bed. They unloaded many things and made a camp there. It wasn't really necessary to make a camp on the ground. There was a good motel two miles away on the highway; there was a road along the ridge above. They could have lived in comfort and made the trip to the site in five minutes every morning. Terrence Burdock, however, believed that one could not get the feel of a digging unless he lived on the ground with it day and night.

The five persons were Terrence Burdock, his wife Ethyl, Robert Derby, and Howard Steinleser: four beautiful and balanced people. And Magdalen Mobley who was neither beautiful nor balanced. But she was electric; she was special. They crouched around in the formations a little after they had made camp and while there was still light. All of them had seen the formations before and had guessed that there was promise in them.

"That peculiar fluting in the broken chimney is almost like a core sample," Terrence said, "and it differs from the rest of it. It's like a lightning bolt through the whole length. It's already exposed for us. I believe we will remove the chimney entirely. It covers the perfect access for the slash in the mound, and it is the mound in which we are really interested. But we'll study the chimney first. It is so available for study."

"Oh, I can tell you everything that's in the chimney," Magdalen said crossly. "I can tell you everything that's in the mound too."

"I wonder why we take the trouble to dig if you already know what we will find," Ethyl sounded archly.

"I wonder too," Magdalen grumbled. "But we will need the evidence and the artifacts to show. You can't get appropriations without evidence and artifacts to show. Robert, go kill that deer in the brush about forty yards northeast of the chimney. We may as well have deer meat if we're living primitive."

"This isn't deer season," Robert Derby objected. "And there isn't any deer there. Or, if there is, it's down in the draw where you couldn't see it. And if there's one there, it's probably a doe."

"No, Robert, it is a two-year-old buck and a very big one. Of course it's in the draw where I can't see it. Forty yards northeast of the chimney would have to be in the draw. If I could see it, the rest of you could see it too. Now go kill it! Are you a man or a *mas microtus*? Howard, cut poles and set up a tripod to string and dress the deer on."

"You had better try the thing, Robert," Ethyl Burdock said, "or we'll have no peace this evening."

Robert Derby took a carbine and went northeastward of the chimney, descending into the draw near at forty yards. There was the high ping of the carbine shot. And, after some moments, Robert returned with a curious grin.

"You didn't miss him, Robert, you killed him," Magdalen called loudly. "You got him with a good shot through the throat and up into the brain when he tossed his head high like they do. Why didn't you bring him? Go back and get him!"

"Get him? I couldn't even lift the thing. Terrence and Howard, come with me and we'll lash it to a pole and get it here somehow."

"Oh, Robert, you're out of your beautiful mind," Magdalen chided. "It only weighs a hundred and ninety pounds. Oh, I'll get it."

Magdalen Mobley went and got the big buck. She brought it back, carrying it listless across her shoulders and getting herself bloodied, stopping sometimes to examine rocks and kick them with her foot, coming easily with her load. It looked as if it might weigh two hundred and fifty pounds; but if Magdalen said it weighed a hundred and ninety, that is what it weighed.

Howard Steinleser had cut poles and made a tripod. He knew better than not to. They strung the buck up, skinned it off, ripped up its belly, drew it, and worked it over in an almost professional manner.

"Cook it, Ethyl," Magdalen said.

Later, as they sat on the ground around the fire and it had turned dark, Ethyl brought the buck's brains to Magdalen, messy and not half cooked, believing that she was playing an evil trick. And Magdalen ate them avidly. They were her due. She had discovered the buck.

If you wonder how Magdalen knew where invisible things were, so did the other members of the party always wonder.

"It bedevils me sometimes why I am the only one to notice the analogy between historical geology and depth psychology," Terrence Burdock mused as they grew lightly profound around the campfire. "The isostatic principle applies to the mind and the under-mind as well as it does to the surface and under-surface of the earth. The mind has its erosions and weatherings going on along with its deposits and accumulations. It also has its upthrusts and its stresses. It floats in a similar magma. In extreme cases it has its volcanic eruptions and its mountain-building."

"And it has its glaciations," Ethyl Burdock said, and perhaps she was looking at her husband in the dark.

"The mind has its hard sandstone, sometimes transmuted to quartz, or half-transmuted into flint, from the drifting and floating sand of daily events. It has its shale from the old mud of daily ineptitudes and inertias. It has limestone out of its more vivid experiences, for lime is the remnant of what was once animate: and this limestone may be true marble if it is the deposit of rich enough emotion, or even travertine if it has bubbled sufficiently through agonized and evocative rivers of the under-mind. The mind has its sulfur and its gemstones—" Terrence bubbled on sufficiently, and Magdalen cut him.

"Say simply that we have rocks in our heads," she said. "But they're random rocks, I tell you, and the same ones keep coming back. It *isn't* the same with us as it is with the earth. The world gets new rocks all the time. But it's the same people who keep turning up, and the same minds. Damn, one of the samest of them just turned up again! I wish he'd leave me alone. The answer is still no."

Very often Magdalen said things that made no sense. Ethyl Burdock assured herself that neither her husband, nor Robert, nor Howard, had slipped over to Magdalen in the dark. Ethyl was jealous of the chunky and surly girl.

"I am hoping that this will be as rich as Spiro Mound," Howard Steinleser hoped. "It could be, you know. I'm told that there was never a less prepossessing site than that, or a trickier one. I wish we had someone who had dug at Spiro."

"Oh, he dug at Spiro," Magdalen said with contempt.

"He? Who?" Terrence Burdock asked. "No one of us was at Spiro. Magdalen, you weren't even born yet when that mound was opened. What could you know about it?"

"Yeah, I remember him at Spiro," Magdalen said, "always turning up his own things and pointing them out."

"*Were* you at Spiro?" Terrence suddenly asked a piece of darkness. For some time, they had all been vaguely aware that there were six, not five, persons around the fire.

"Yeah, I was at Spiro," the man said. "I dig there. I dig at a lot of the digs. I dig real well, and I always know when we come to something that will be important. You give me a job."

"Who are you?" Terrence asked him. The man was pretty visible now. The flame of the fire seemed to lean towards him as if he compelled it.

"Oh, I'm just a rich old poor man who keeps following and hoping and asking. There is *one* who is worth it all forever, so I solicit that one forever. And sometimes I am other things. Two hours ago I was the deer in the draw. It is an odd thing to munch one's own flesh." And the man was munching a joint of the deer, unasked.

"Him and his damn cheap poetry!" Magdalen cried angrily.

"What's your name?" Terrence asked him.

"Manypenny. Anteros Manypenny is my name forever."

"What are you?"

"Oh, just Indian. Shawnee, Choc, Creek, Anadarko, Caddo, and pre-Caddo. Lots of things."

"How could anyone be pre-Caddo?"

"Like me. I am."

"Is Anteros a Creek name?"

"No. Greek. Man, I am a going Jessie, I am one digging man! I show you tomorrow."

Four more hoe cuts, and Anteros *did* come to them. He uncovered two large points and one small one, spear heads and arrowhead. Lanceolate they were, with ribbon flaking. They were late Folsom, or they were proto-Plano; they were what you will.

"This cannot be," Steinleser groaned. "They're the missing chips, the transition pieces. They fill the missing places too well. I won't believe it. I'd hardly believe it if mastodon bones were found on the same level here."

"In a moment," said Anteros, beginning to use the hoe again. "Hey, those old beasts *did smell funny!* An elephant isn't in it with them. And a lot of it still clings to their bones. Will a sixth thoracic bone do? I'm pretty sure that's what it is. I don't know where the rest of the animal is. Probably somebody gnawed the thoracic here. Nine hoe cuts, and then very careful."

Nine hoe cuts; and then Anteros, using a mason's trowel, unearthed the old gnawed bone very carefully. Yes, Howard said almost angrily, it was a sixth thoracic of a mastodon. Robert Derby said it was a fifth or sixth; it is not easy to tell.

"Leave the digging for a while, Anteros," Steinleser said. "I want to record and photograph and take a few measurements here."

Terrence Burdock and Magdalen Mobley were working at the bottom of the chimney rock, at the bottom of the fluting that ran the whole height of it like a core sample.

"Get Anteros over here and see what he can uncover in sixty seconds," Terrence offered.

"Oh him! He'll just uncover some of his own things."

"What do you mean, his own things? Nobody could have made an intrusion here. It's hard sandstone."

"And harder flint here," Magdalen said. "I might have known it. Pass the damned thing up. I know just about what it says anyhow."

"What it says? What do you mean? But it is marked! And it's large and dressed rough. Who'd carve in flint?"

"Somebody real stubborn, just like flint," Magdalen said. "All right then, let's have it out. Anteros! Get this out in one piece. And do it without shattering it or tumbling the whole thing down on us. He can do it, you know, Terrence. He can do things like that."

"What do you know about his doings, Magdalen? You never saw or heard about the poor man till last night."

"Oh well, I know that it'll turn out to be the same damned stuff."

Anteros did get it out without shattering it or bringing down the chimney column. A cleft with a digging bar, three sticks of the stuff and a cap, and he touched the leads to the battery when he was almost on top of the charge. The blast, it sounded as if the whole sky were falling down on them, and some of those sky-blocks were quite large stones. The ancients wondered why fallen pieces of the sky should always be dark rock-stuff and never sky-blue clear stuff. The answer is that it is only pieces of the night sky that ever fall, even though they may sometimes be most of the daytime in falling, such is the distance. And the blast that Anteros set off did bring down rocky hunks of the night sky even though it was broad daylight. They brought down darker rocks than any of which the chimney was composed.

Still, it was a small blast. The chimney tottered but did not collapse. It settled back uneasily on its base. And the flint block was out in the clear.

"A thousand spear-heads and arrowheads could be shattered and chipped out of that hunk," Terrence marveled. "That flint block would have been a primitive fortune for a primitive man."

"I had several such fortunes," Anteros said dully, "and this one I preserved and dedicated."

They had all gathered around it.

"Oh the poor man!" Ethyl suddenly exclaimed, but she was not looking at any of the men. She was looking at the stone.

"I wish he'd get off that kick," Magdalen sputtered angrily. "I don't care *how* rich he is. I can pick up better stuff than him in the alleys."

"What are the women chirping about?" Terrence asked. "But those do look like true glyphs. Almost like Aztec, are they not, Steinleser?"

"Nahust-Tanoan, cousins-german to the Aztec, or should I say cousins-yaqui?"

"Call it anything, but can you read it?"

"Probably. Give me eight or ten hours on it and I should come up with a contingent reading of many of the glyphs. We can hardly expect a rational rendering of the message, however. All Nahust-Tanoan translations so far have been gibberish."

"And remember, Terrence, that Steinleser is a slow reader," Magdalen said spitefully. "And he isn't very good at interpreting *other* signs either."

Steinleser was sullen and silent. How had his face come to bear those deep livid claw marks today?

They moved a lot of rock and rubble that morning, took quite a few pictures, wrote up bulky notes. There were constant finds as the divided party worked up the shag-slash in the mound and the core-flute of the chimney. There were no more really startling discoveries; no more turned pots of the proto-Plano period; how could there be? There were no more predicted and perfect points of the late Folsom, but there were broken and unpredictable points. No other mastodon thoracic was found, but bones were uncovered of *bison latifrons,* of dire wolf, of coyote, of man. There were some anomalies in the relationship of the things discovered, but it was not as fishy as it had been in the early morning, not as fishy as when Anteros had announced and then dug out the shards of the pot, the three points, the mastodon bone. The things now were as authentic as they expected, and yet their very profusion had still the smell of a small fish.

And that Anteros was one digging man. He moved sand, he moved the stone, he missed nothing. And at noon he disappeared.

An hour later he reappeared in a glossy station wagon, coming out of a thicketed ravine where no one would have expected a way. He had been to town. He brought a variety of cold cuts, cheeses, relishes and pastries, a couple of cases of cold beer, and some V.O.

"I thought you were a poor man, Anteros," Terrence chided.

"I told you that I was a rich old poor man. I have nine thousand acres of grassland, I have three thousand head of cattle, I have alfalfa land and clover land and corn land and hay-grazer land—"

"Oh, knock it off!" Magdalen snapped.

"I have other things," Anteros finished sullenly.

They ate, they rested, they worked the afternoon. Magdalen worked as swiftly and solidly as did Anteros. She was young, she was stocky, she was light-burned-dark. She was not at all beautiful (Ethyl was). She could have any man there any time she wanted to (Ethyl couldn't). She was Magdalen, the often unpleasant, the mostly casual, the suddenly intense one. She was the tension of the party, the string of the bow.

"Anteros!" she called sharply just at sundown.

"The turtle?" he asked. "The turtle that is under the ledge out of the current where the backwater curls in reverse? But he is fat and happy and he has never harmed anything except for food or fun. I know you do not want me to get that turtle."

"I do! There's eighteen pounds of him. He's fat. He'll be good. Only eighty yards, where the bank crumbles down to Green River, under the lower ledge that's shale that looks like slate, two feet deep—"

"I know where he is. I will go get the fat turtle," Anteros said. "I myself am the fat turtle. I am the Green River." He went to get it.

"Oh that damned poetry of his!" Magdalen spat when he was gone.

Anteros brought back the fat turtle. He looked as if he'd

weigh twenty-five pounds; but if Magdalen said he weighed eighteen pounds, then it was eighteen.

"Start cooking, Ethyl," Magdalen said. Magdalen was a mere undergraduate girl permitted on the digging by sheer good fortune. The others of the party were archaeologists of the moment. Magdalen had no right to give orders to anyone, except her born right.

"I don't know how to cook a turtle," Ethyl complained.

"Anteros will show you how."

"The late evening smell of newly exposed excavation!" Terrence Burdock burbled as they lounged around the campfire a little later, full of turtle and V.O. and feeling rakishly wise. "The exposed age can be guessed by the very timbre of the smell, I believe."

And, indeed, there was something time-evocative about the smell of the diggings; cool, at the same time musty and musky, ripe with old stratified water and compressed death. Stratified time.

"It helps if you already know what the exposed age is," said Howard Steinleser. "Here there is an anomaly. The chimney sometimes acts as if it were younger than the mound. The chimney cannot be young enough to include written rock, but it is."

"Archaeology is made up entirely of anomalies, rearranged to fit," said Robert Derby. "Have you unriddled the glyph-stone, Howard?"

"Yes, pretty well. Better than I expected. Charles August can verify it, of course, when we get it back to the university. It is a non-royal, non-tribal, non-warfare, non-hunt declaration. It does not come under any of the usual radical signs, any of the categories. It can only be categorized as uncategorized or personal. The translation will be rough."

"Rocky is the word," said Magdalen.

"On with it, Howard," Ethyl cried.

"'You are the freedom of wild pigs in the sour grass, and the nobility of badgers. You are the brightness of serpents and the soaring of vultures. You are passion of mesquite bushes on fire with lightning. You are the serenity of toads.'"

"You've got to admit he's got a different line," said Ethyl. "Your own love notes were less acrid, Terrence."

"What kind of thing is it, Steinleser?" Terrence questioned. "It must have a category."

"I believe Ethyl is right. It's a love poem. 'You are the water in rock cisterns and the secret spiders in that water. You are the dead coyote lying half in the stream, and you are the old entrapped dreams of the coyote's brains oozing liquid through the broken eye socket. You are the happy ravening flies about that broken socket.'"

"Oh, hold it, Steinleser," Robert Derby cried. "You can't have gotten all that from scratches on flint. What is 'entrapped dreams' in Nahuat-Tanoan glyph-writing?"

"The solid-person sign next to the hollow-person sign, both enclosed in the night sign—that has always been interpreted as the dream glyph. And here the dream glyph is enclosed in the glyph of the deadfall trap. Yes, I believe it means entrapped dreams. To continue: 'You are the corn worm in the dark heart of the corn, the naked small bird in the nest. You are the pustules on the sick rabbit, devouring life and flesh and turning it into your own serum. You are stars compressed into charcoal. But you cannot give, you cannot take. Once again you will be broken at the foot of the cliff, and the word will remain unsaid in your purple and swollen tongue.'"

"A love poem, perhaps, but with a difference," said Robert Derby.

"I never was able to go for his stuff and I tried, I really tried," Magdalen moaned.

"Here is the change of person-subject shown by the canted-eye glyph linked with the self-glyph," Steinleser explained. "It is now a first-person talk. 'I own ten thousand back-loads of corn. I own gold and beans and nine buffalo horns full of watermelon seeds. I own the loincloth that the sun wore on his fourth journey across the sky. Only three loincloths in the world are older and more valued than this. I cry out to you in a big voice like the hammering of herons' (that sound-verb-particle is badly translated, the hammer being not a modern pounding hammer but a rock angling, chipping hammer) 'and the belching of buffaloes. My love is sinewy as entwined snakes, it is steadfast as the sloth, it is like a feathered arrow shot into your abdomen—such is my love. Why is my love unrequited?'"

"I challenge you, Steinleser," Terrence Burdock cut in. "What is the glyph for 'unrequited'?"

"The glyph of the extended hand—with all the fingers bent backwards. It goes on: 'I roar to you. Do not throw yourself down. You believe you are on the hanging sky bridge, but you are on the terminal cliff. I grovel before you. I am no more than dog-dropping.'"

"You'll notice he said that and not me," Magdalen burst out. There was always a fundamental incoherence about Magdalen.

"Ah—continue, Steinleser," said Terrence. "The girl is daft, or she dreams out loud."

"That is all of the inscriptions, Terrence, except for the final glyph which I don't understand. Glyph writing takes a lot of room. That's all the stone would hold."

"What is the glyph you don't understand, Howard?"

"It's the spear thrower glyph entwined with the time glyph. It sometimes means 'flung forward or beyond.' But what does it mean here?"

"It means 'continued,' dummy. 'Continued,'" Magdalen said. "Do not fear. There'll be more stones."

"I think it's beautiful," said Ethyl Burdock, "—in its own context, of course."

"Then why don't you take him on, Ethyl, in his own context, of course?" Magdalen asked. "Myself, I don't care how many back-loads of corn he owns. I've had it."

"Take whom on, dear?" Ethyl asked. "Howard Steinleser can interpret the stones, but who can interpret our Magdalen?"

"Oh, I can read her like a rock," Terrence Burdock smiled. But he couldn't.

But it had fastened on them. It was all about them and through them: the brightness of serpents and the serenity of toads, the secret spiders in the water, the entrapped dreams oozing through the broken eye socket, the pustules of the sick rabbit, the belching of buffalo, and the arrow shot into the abdomen. And around it all was the night smell of lint and turned earth and chuckling streams, the mustiness, and the special muskiness which bears the name Nobility of Badgers.

They talked archaeology and myth talk. Then it was steep night, and the morning of the third day.

Oh, the sample digging went well. This was already a richer mound than Spiro, though the gash in it was but a small promise of things to come. And the curious twin of the mound, the broken chimney, confirmed and confounded and contradicted. There was time gone wrong in the chimney, or at least in the curious fluted core of it; the rest of it was normal enough, and sterile enough.

Anteros worked that day with a soft sullenness, and Magdalen brooded with a sort of lightning about her.

"Beads, glass beads!" Terrence Burdock exploded angrily. "All right! Who is the hoaxer in our midst? I will not tolerate this at all." Terrence had been angry of face all day. He was clawed deeply, as Steinleser had been the day before, and he was sour on the world.

"There have been glass bead caches before, Terrence, hundreds of them," Robert Derby said softly.

"There have been hoaxers before, hundreds of them," Terrence howled. "These have 'Hong Kong Contemporary' written all over them, damn cheap glass beads sold by the pound. They have no business in a stratum of around the year seven hundred. All right, who is guilty?"

"I don't believe that any one of us is guilty, Terrence," Ethyl put in mildly. "They are found four feet in from the slant surface of the mound. Why, we've cut through three hundred years of vegetable loam to get to them, and certainly the surface was eroded beyond that."

"We are scientists," said Steinleser. "We find these. Others have found such. Let us consider the improbabilities of it."

It was noon, so they ate and rested and considered the improbabilities. Anteros had brought them a great joint of white pork, and they made sandwiches and drank beer and ate pickles.

"You know," said Robert Derby, "that beyond the rank impossibility of glass beads found so many times where they

142

could not be found, there is a real mystery about *all* early Indian beads, whether of bone, stone, or antler. There are millions and millions of these fine beads with pierced holes finer than any piercer ever found. There are residues, there are centers of every other Indian industry, and there is evolution of every other tool. Why have there been these millions of pierced beads, and never one piercer? There was no technique to make so fine a piercer. How were they done?"

Magdalen giggled. "Bead-spitter," she said.

"Bead-spitter! You're out of your fuzzy mind," Terrence erupted. "That's the silliest and least sophisticated of all Indian legends."

"But it *is* the legend," said Robert Derby, "the legend of more than thirty separate tribes. The Carib Indians of Cuba said that they got their beads from Bead-spitters. The Indians of Panama told Balboa the same thing. The Indians of the pueblos told the same story to Coronado. Every Indian community had an Indian who was its Bead-spitter. There are Creek and Alabama and Kaosati stories of Bead-spitters; see Swanson's collections. And his stories were taken down within living memory.

"More than that, when European trade beads were first introduced, there is one account of an Indian receiving some and saying 'I will take some to Bead-spitter. If he sees them, he can spit them too.' And that Bead-spitter did then spit them by the bushel. There was never any other Indian account of the origin of their beads. *All* were spit by a Bead-spitter."

"Really, this is very unreal," Ethyl said. Really it was.

"Hog hokey! A Bead-spitter of around the year seven hundred could not spit future beads, he could not spit cheap Hong Kong glass beads of the present time!" Terrence was very angry.

"Pardon me, yes, he could," said Anteros. "A Bead-spit-ter can spit future beads, if he faces north when he spits. That has always been known."

Terrence was angry, he fumed and poisoned the day for them, and the claw marks on his face stood out livid purple. He was angrier yet when he said that the curious dark cap-ping rock on top of the chimney was dangerous, that it would fall and kill someone; and Anteros said that there was no such capping rock on the chimney, that Terrence's eyes were deceiv-ing him, that Terrence should go sit in the shade and rest.

And Terrence became excessively angry when he dis-covered that Magdalen was trying to hide something she had discovered in the fluted core of the chimney. It was a large and heavy shale-stone, too heavy even for Magdalen's puzzling strength. She had dragged it out of the chimney flute, tumbled it down to the bottom, and was trying to cover it with rocks and scarp.

"Robert, mark the extraction point!" Terrence called loudly. "It's quite plain yet. Magdalen, stop that! Whatever it is, it must be examined now."

"Oh, it's just more of the damned same thing! I wish he'd let me alone. With his kind of money he can get plenty of girls. Besides, it's private, Terrence. You don't have any busi-ness reading it."

"You are hysterical, Magdalen, and you may have to leave the digging site."

"I wish I could leave. I can't. I wish I could love. I can't. Why isn't it enough that I die?"

"Howard, spend the afternoon on this," Terrence ordered. "It has writing of a sort on it. If it's what I think it is, it scares me. It's too recent to be in any eroded chimney rock forma-tion, Howard, and it comes from far below the top. Read it."

"A few hours on it and I may come up with something. I never saw anything like it either. What do you think it was, Terrence?"

"What do you think I think it is? It's much later than the other, and that one was impossible. I'll not be the one to confess myself crazy first."

Howard Steinleser went to work on the incised stone; and two hours before sundown they brought him another one, a gray soapstone block from higher up. Whatever this was covered with, it was not at all the same thing that covered the shale-stone.

And elsewhere things went well, too well. The old fishiness was back on it. No series of finds could be so perfect, no petrification could be so well ordered.

"Robert," Magdalen called down to Robert Derby just at sunset, "in the meadow above the shore, about four hundred yards down, just past the old fence—"

"—there is a badger hole, Magdalen. Now you have me doing it, seeing invisible things at a distance. And if I take a carbine and stroll down there quietly, the badger will stick his head out just as I get there (I being strongly downwind of him), and I'll blam him between the eyes. He'll be a big one, fifty pounds."

"Thirty. Bring him, Robert. You're showing a little understanding at last."

"But, Magdalen, badger is rampant meat. It's seldom eaten."

"May not the condemned girl have what she wishes for her last meal? Go get it, Robert."

Robert went. The voice of the little carbine was barely heard at that distance. Soon, Robert brought back the dead badger.

"Cook it, Ethyl," Magdalen ordered.

"Yes, I know. And if I don't know how, Anteros will show me." But Anteros was gone. Robert found him on a sun-down knoll with his shoulders hunched. The odd man was sobbing silently and his face seemed to be made out of dull pumice stone. But he came back to aid Ethyl in preparing the badger.

"If the first of today's stone scared you, the second should have lifted the hair right off your head, Terrence," Howard Steinleser said.

"It does, it does. All the stones are too recent to be in a chimney formation, but this last one is an insult. It isn't two hundred years old, but there's a thousand years of strata above it. What time is deposited there?"

They had eaten rampant badger meat and drunk inferior whiskey (which Anteros, who had given it to them, didn't know was inferior), and the muskiness was both inside them and around them. The campfire sometimes spit angrily with small explosions, and its glare reached high when it did so. By one such leaping glare, Terrence Burdock saw that the curious dark capping rock was once more on the top of the chimney. He thought he had seen it there in the daytime; but it had not been there after he had set in the shade and rested, and it had absolutely not been there when he climbed the chimney itself to be sure.

"Let's have the second chapter and then the third, Howard," Ethyl said. "It's neater that way."

"Yes, tell, the second chapter (the first and the lowest apparently the earliest rock we came on today) is written in a language that no one ever saw written before; and yet it's no great trouble to read it. Even Terrence guessed what it was and it scared him. It is Anadarko-Caddo hand-talk graven in stone. It is what is called the sign language of the Plains Indians copied down in formalized pictograms. And it *has* to be very recent, within the last three hundred years. Hand-talk was fragmentary at the first coming of the Spanish, and well developed at the first coming of the French. It was an explosive development, as such things go, worked out within a hundred years. This rock has to be younger than its *situs*, but it was absolutely found in place."

"Read it, Howard, read it," Robert Derby called. Robert was feeling fine and the rest of them were gloomy tonight.

"'I own three hundred ponies,'" Steinleser read the rock out of his memory. "'I own two days' ride north and east and south, and one day's ride west. I give you all. I blast out with a big voice like fire in tall trees, like the explosion of crowning pine trees. I cry like closing-in wolves, like the high voice of the lion, like the hoarse scream of torn calves. Do you not destroy yourself again! You are the dew on crazy weed in the morning. You are the swift crooked wings of the nighthawk, the dainty feet of the skunk, you are the juice of the sour squash. Why can you not take or give? I am the humpbacked bull of the high plains, I am the river itself and the stagnant pools left by the river, I am the raw earth and the rocks. Come to me, but do not come so violently as to destroy yourself.'

"Ah, that was the text of the first rock of the day, the Anadarko-Caddo hand-talk graven in stone. And final pictograms which I don't understand: a shot arrow sign, and a boulder beyond."

"'Continued on next rock' of course," said Robert Derby. "Well, why *wasn't* hand-talk ever written down? The signs

147

are simple and easily stylized and they were understood by many different tribes. It would have been natural to write it."

"Alphabetical writing was in the region *before* hand-talk was well developed," Terrence Burdock said. "In fact, it was the coming of the Spanish that gave the impetus to hand-talk. It was really developed for communication between Spanish and Indian, not between Indian and Indian. And yet, I believe, hand-talk *was* written down once; it was the beginning of the Chinese pictographs. And there also it had its beginning as communication between differing peoples. Depend on it, if all mankind had always been of a single language, there would never have been any written language at all. Writing always began as a bridge, and there had to be some chasm for it to bridge."

"We have one to bridge here," said Steinleser. "The whole chimney is full of rotten smoke. The highest part of it should be older than the lowest part of the mound, since the mound was built on a base eroded away from the chimney formation. But in many ways they seem to be contemporary. We must all be under a spell here. We've worked two days on this, parts of three days, and the total impossibility of the situation hasn't struck us yet.

"The old Nahuatlan glyphs for time are the chimney glyphs. Present time is a lower part of chimney and fire burning at the base. Past time is black smoke from a chimney, and future time is white smoke from a chimney. There was a signature glyph running through our yesterday's stone which I didn't and don't understand. It seemed to indicate something coming down out of the chimney rather than going up it."

"It really doesn't look much like a chimney," Magdalen said.

"And a maiden doesn't look much like dew on crazy weed in the morning, Magdalen," Robert Derby said, "but we recognize these identities."

They talked a while about the impossibility of the whole business.

"There are scales on our eyes," Steinleser said. "The fluted core of the chimney is wrong. I'm not even sure the rest of the chimney is right."

"No, it isn't," said Robert Derby. "We can identify most of the strata of the chimney with known periods of the river and stream. I was above and below today. There is one stretch where the sandstone was not eroded at all, where it stands three hundred yards back from the shifted river and is overlaid with a hundred years of loam and sod. There are other sections where the stone is cut away variously. We can tell when most of the chimney was laid down; we can find its correspondences up to a few hundred years ago. But when were the top ten feet of it laid down? There were no correspondences anywhere to that. The centuries represented by the strata of the top of the chimney, people, those centuries haven't happened yet."

"And when was the dark capping rock on top of it all formed—?" Terrence began. "Ah, I'm out of my mind. It isn't there. I'm demented."

"No more than the rest of us," said Steinleser. "I saw it too, I thought, today. And then I didn't see it again."

"The rock writing, it's like an old novel that I only half remember," said Ethyl.

"Oh, that's what it is, yes," Magdalen murmured.

"But I don't remember what happened to the girl in it."

"*I* remember what happened to her, Ethyl," Magdalen said.

"Give us the third chapter, Howard," Ethyl asked. "I want to see how it comes out."

"First you should all have whiskey for those colds," Anteros suggested humbly.

"But none of us have colds," Ethyl objected.

"You take your own medicinal advice, Ethyl, and I'll take mine," Terrence said. "I will have whiskey. My cold is not rheum but fear-chill."

They all had whiskey. They talked a while, and some of them dozed.

"It's late, Howard," Ethyl said after a while. "Let's have the next chapter. Is it the last chapter? Then we'll sleep. We have honest digging to do tomorrow."

"Our third stone, our second stone of just past, is another and even later form of writing, and it has never been seen in stone before. It is Kiowa picture writing. The Kiowas did their out-turning spiral writing on buffalo skins dressed almost as fine as vellum. In its more sophisticated form (and this is a copy of that) it is quite late. The Kiowa picture writing probably did not arrive at its excellence until influenced by White artists."

"How late, Steinleser?" Robert Derby asked.

"Not more than a hundred and fifty years old. But I have never seen it copied in stone before. It simply isn't stone-styled. There's a lot of things around here lately that I haven't seen before.

"Well then, to the text, or should I say the pictography? 'You fear the earth, you fear rough ground and rocks, you fear moister earth and rotting flesh, you fear the flesh itself, all flesh is rotting flesh. If you love not rotting flesh, you love not at all. You believe the bridge hanging in the sky, the bridge hung by tendrils and woody vines that diminish as they go and up till they are no thicker than hairs. There is no sky bridge, you cannot go upon it. Did you believe that the roots of love grow upside down? They come out of deep earth that is old flesh and brains and hearts and entrails, that is old buffalo bowels and snakes' pizzles, that is black blood and rot and moaning underground. This is old and worn-out and bloody Time, and the roots of love grow out of its gore.'"

"You seem to give remarkable detailed translations of the simple pictures, Steinleser, but I begin to get in the mood of it," Terrence said.

"Ah, perhaps I cheat a little," said Steinleser.

"You lie a lot," Magdalen challenged.

"No I do not. There is some basis for every phrase I've used. It goes on: 'I own twenty-two trade rifles. I own ponies. I own Mexico silver, eight-bit pieces. I am rich in all ways. I give all to you. I cry out with big voice like a bear full of mad weed, like a bullfrog in love, like a stallion rearing against a puma. It is the earth that calls you. I am the earth, woollier than wolves and rougher than rocks. I am the bog earth that sucks you in. You cannot give, you cannot take, you cannot love, you think there is something else, you think there is a sky bridge you may loiter on without crashing down. I am bristle boar earth, there is no other. You will come to me in the morning. You will come to me easy and with grace. Or you will come to me reluctant and you be shattered in every bone and member of you. You be broken by our encounter. You be shattered as by a lightning bolt striking up from the earth. I am the red calf which is in the writings. I am the rotting red earth. Live in the morning or die in the morning, but remember that love in death is better than no love at all.'"

"Oh brother! Nobody gets that stuff from kid pictures, Steinleser," Robert Derby moaned.

"Ah well, that's the end of the spiral picture. And a Kiowa spiral pictograph ends with either an in-sweep or an out-sweep. This ends with an out-sweep, which means—"

"'Continued on next rock,' that's what it means," Terrence cried roughly.

"You won't find the next rocks," Magdalen said. "They're hidden, and most of the time they're not there yet, but they will go on and on. But for all that, you'll read it in the rocks tomorrow morning. I want it to be over with. Oh, I don't know what I want!"

"I believe I know what you want tonight, Magdalen," Robert Derby said.

But he didn't.

The talk trailed off, the fire burned down, they went to their sleeping sacks.

Then it was long jagged night, and the morning of the fourth day. But wait! In Nahuat-Tanoan legend, the world ends on the fourth morning. All the lives we lived or thought we lived had been but dreams of the third night. The loincloth that the sun wore on the fourth day's journey was not so valuable as one has made out. It was worn for no more than an hour or so.

And, in fact, there was something terminal about fourth morning. Anteros had disappeared. Magdalen had disappeared. The chimney rock looked greatly diminished in its bulk (something had gone out of it) and much crazier in its broken height. The sun had come up a garish gray-orange color through the fog. The signature glyph of the first stone dominated the ambient. It was as if something were coming down from the chimney, a horrifying smoke; but it was only noisome morning fog.

No it wasn't. There was something else coming down from the chimney, or from the hidden sky: pebbles, stones, indescribable bits of foul oozings, the less fastidious pieces of sky; a light nightmare rain had begun to fall there; the chimney was apparently beginning to crumble.

"It's the damnedest thing I ever heard about," Robert Derby growled. "Do you think that Magdalen really went off with Anteros?" Derby was bitter and fumatory this morning and his face was badly clawed.

"Who is Magdalen? Who is Anteros?" Ethyl Burdock asked.

Terrence Burdock was hooting from high on the mound. "All come up," he called. "Here is a find that will make it all worthwhile. We'll have to photo and sketch and measure and record and witness. It's the finest basalt head I've ever seen, man-sized, and I suspect that there's a man-sized body attached to it. We'll soon clean it and clear it. Gah! What a weird fellow he was!"

But Howard Steinleser was studying a brightly colored something that he held in his two hands.

"What is it, Howard? What are you doing?" Derby demanded.

"Ah, I believe this is the next stone in the sequence. The writing is alphabetical but deformed; there is an element missing. I believe it is in modern English, and I will solve the deformity and see it true in a minute. The text of it seems to be—"

Rocks and stones were coming down from the chimney, and fog, amnesiac and wit-stealing fog.

"Steinleser, are you all right?" Robert Derby asked with compassion. "That isn't a stone that you hold in your hand."

"It isn't a stone. I thought it was. What is it then?"

"It is the fruit of the Osage orange tree, the American *Meraceous*. It isn't a stone, Howard." And the thing was a tough, woody, wrinkled mock-orange, as big as a small melon.

"You have to admit that the wrinkles look a little bit like writing, Robert."

"Yes, they look a little like writing, Howard. Let us go up where Terrence is bawling for us. You've read too many stones. And it isn't safe here."

"Why go up, Howard? The other thing is coming down."

It was the bristle boar earth reaching up with a rumble. It was a lightning bolt struck upward out of the earth, and it got its prey. There was explosion and roar. The dark capping rock was jerked from the top of the chimney and slammed with terrible force to the earth, shattering with a great shock. And something else that had been on that capping rock. And the whole chimney collapsed about them.

She was broken by the encounter. She was shattered in every bone and member of her. And she was dead.

"Who—who is she?" Howard Steinleser stuttered.

"Oh God! Magdalen, of course!" Robert Derby cried.

"I remember her a little bit. Didn't understand her. She put out like an evoking moth but she wouldn't be had. Near clawed the face off me the other night when I misunderstood the signals. She believed there was a sky bridge. It's in a lot of the mythologies. But there isn't one, you know. Oh well."

"The girl is dead! Damnation! What are you grubbing in those stones?"

"Maybe she isn't dead in them yet, Robert. I'm going to read what's here before something happens to them. This capping rock that fell and broke, it's impossible, of course. It's a stratum that hasn't been laid down yet. I always did want to read the future and I may never get another chance."

"You fool! The girl's dead! Does nobody care? Terrence, stop bellowing about your find. Come down. The girl's dead."

"Come up, Robert and Howard," Terrence insisted. "Leave that broken stuff down there. It's worthless. But nobody ever saw anything like this."

"Do come up, men," Ethyl sang. "Oh, it's a wonderful place! I never saw anything like it in my life."

"Ethyl, is the whole morning mad?" Robert Derby demanded as he came up to her. "She's dead. Don't you really remember her? Don't you remember Magdalen?"

"I'm not sure. Is she the girl down there? Isn't she the same girl who's been hanging around here a couple days? She shouldn't have been playing on that high rock. I'm sorry she's dead. But just look what we're uncovering here!"

"Terrence. Don't *you* remember Magdalen?"

"The girl down there? She's a little bit like the girl that clawed the hell out of me the other night. Next time someone goes to town they might mention to the sheriff that there's a dead girl here. Robert, did you ever see a face like this one? And it digs away to reveal the shoulders. I believe there's a whole man-sized figure here. Wonderful, wonderful!"

"Terrence, you're off your head. Well, do you remember Anteros?"

"Certainly, the twin of Eros, but nobody ever made much of the symbol of unsuccessful love. Thunder! That's the name for him! It fits him perfectly. We'll call him Anteros."

Well, it *was* Anteros, life-like in basalt stone. His face contorted. He was sobbing soundlessly and frozenly and his shoulders were hunched with emotion. The carving was fascinating in its miserable passion, his stony love unrequited. Perhaps he was more impressive now than he would be when he was cleaned. He was earth, he was earth itself. Whatever period the carving belonged to, it was outstanding in its power.

"The live Anteros, Terrence. Don't you remember our digging man, Anteros Manypenny?"

"Sure. Didn't show up for work this morning, did he? Tell him he's fired."

"Magdalen is dead! She was one of us! Damn it, she was the main one of us!" Robert Derby cried. Terrence and Ethyl were earless to his outburst. They were busy uncovering the rest of the carving.

And down below, Howard Steinleser was studying dark broken rocks before they would disappear, studying a stratum that hadn't been laid down yet, reading a foggy future.

DIARY OF A GOD

Barry Pain

First published in *Stories in the Dark*, 1901

Barry Pain's "Diary of a God" is one of many to use the device of a found journal to create the immediacy of first person narration without bringing us face to face with someone we might not really want to meet. In this case, we are privy to the narrator's deification, and to the creation of a new pantheon of gods.

During the week there had been several thunderstorms. It was after the last of these, on a cool Saturday evening, that he was found at the top of the hill by a shepherd. His speech was incoherent and disconnected; he gave his name correctly, but could or would add no account of himself. He was wet through, and sat there pulling a sprig of heather to pieces. The shepherd afterwards said that he had great difficulty in persuading him to come down, and that he talked nonsense. In the path at the foot of the hill he was recognized by some people from the farmhouse where he was lodging, and was taken back there. They had, indeed, gone out to look for him. He was subsequently removed to an asylum, and died insane a few months later.

Two years afterwards, when the furniture of the farmhouse came to be sold by auction, there was found in a little cupboard in the bedroom which he had occupied an ordinary penny exercise book. This was partly filled, in a beautiful and very regular handwriting, with what seems to have been something in the nature of a diary, and the following are extracts from it:

June 1st—It is absolutely essential to be quiet. I am beginning life again, and in quite a different way, and on quite a different scale, and I cannot make the break suddenly. I must have a pause of a few weeks in between the two different lives. I saw the advertisement of the lodgings in this farmhouse in an evening paper that somebody had left at the restaurant. That was when I was trying to make the change abruptly, and I may as well make note of what happened.

After attending the funeral (which seemed to me an act of hypocrisy, as I hardly knew the man, but it was expected of me) I came back to my Charlotte Street rooms and had tea. I slept well that night. Then the next morning I went to the office at the usual hour, in my best clothes, and with a deep band still on my hat. I went to Mr. Toller's room and knocked. He said, "Come in," and after I had entered: "Can I do anything for you? What do you want?"

Then I explained to him that I wished to leave at once. He said:

"This seems sudden, after thirty years' service."

"Yes," I replied. "I have served you faithfully for thirty years, but things have changed, and I have now three hundred a year of my own. I will pay something in lieu of notice, if you like, but I cannot go on being a clerk any more. I hope, Mr. Toller, you will not think that I speak with any impertinence to yourself, or any immodesty, but I am really in the position of a private gentleman."

He looked at me curiously, and as he did not say anything I repeated:

"I think I am in the position of a private gentleman."

In the end he let me go, and said very politely he was sorry to lose me. I said goodbye to the other clerks, even to those who had sometimes laughed at what they imagined to be my peculiarities. I gave the better of the two office boys a small present in money.

I went back to the Charlotte Street rooms, but there was nothing to do there. There were figures going on in my head, and my fingers seemed to be running up and down columns. I had a stupid idea that I should be in trouble if Mr. Toller were to come in and catch me like that. I went out and had a capital lunch, and then I went to the theater. I took a stall right in the front row, and sat there all by myself. Then I had a cab to the restaurant. It was too soon for dinner, so I ordered a whiskey and soda, and smoked a few cigarettes. The man at the table next to me left the evening paper in which I saw the advertisement of these farmhouse lodgings. I read the whole of the paper, but I have forgotten it all except that advertisement, and I could say it by heart now—all about bracing air and perfect quiet and the rest of it. For dinner I had a bottle of champagne. The waiter handed me a list, and asked which I would prefer. I waved the list away and said:

"Give me the best."

He smiled. He kept on smiling all through dinner until the end; then he looked serious. He kept getting more serious. Then he brought two other men to look at me. They spoke to me, but I did not want to talk. I think I fell asleep.

I found myself in my rooms in Charlotte Street next morning, and my landlady gave me notice because, she said, I had come home beastly drunk. Then that advertisement flashed into my mind about the bracing air. I said:

"I should have given you notice in any case; this is not a suitable place for a gentleman."

June 3rd—I am rather sorry that I wrote down the above. It seems so degrading. However, it was merely an act of ignorance and carelessness on my part, and, besides, I am writing solely for myself. To myself I may own freely that I made a mistake, that I was not used to the wine, and that I had not fully gauged what the effects would be. The incident is disgusting, but I simply put it behind me, and think no more about it. I pay here two pounds ten shillings a week for my two rooms and board. I take my meals, of course, by myself in the sitting room. It would be rather cheaper if I took them with the family, but I do not care about that. After all, what is two pounds ten shillings a week? Roughly speaking, a hundred and thirty pounds a year.

June 17th—I have made no entry in my diary for some days. For a certain period I have had no heart for that or anything else. I had told the people here that I was a private gentleman (which is strictly true), and that I was engaged in literary pursuits. By the latter I meant to imply no more than that I am fond of reading, and that it is my intention to jot down from time to time my sensations and experiences in the new life which has burst upon me. At the same time I have been greatly depressed. Why, I can hardly explain. I have been furious with myself. Sitting in my own sitting room, with a gold-tipped cigarette between my fingers, I have been possessed (even though I recognized it as an absurdity) by a feeling that if Mr. Toller were to come in suddenly I should get up and apologize. But the thing which depressed me most was the open country. I have read, of course, those penny stories about the poor little ragged boys who never see the green leaf in their lives, and I always thought them exaggerated. So they are exaggerated: there are the Embankment Gardens with the Press Band playing; there are parks; there are Sunday school treats. All these little ragged boys see the green leaf, and to say they do not is an exaggeration—I am afraid a willful exaggeration. But to see the open country is quite a different thing. Yesterday was a fine day, and I was out all day in a place called Wensley Dale. On one spot where I stood I could see for miles all around. There was not a single house, or tree, or human being in sight. There was just myself on top of a moor; the bigness of it gave me a regular scare. I suppose I had got used to walls: I had got used to feeling that if I went straight ahead without stopping I should knock against something. That somehow made me feel safe. Out on that great moor— just as if I were the last man left alive in the world—I do not feel safe. I find the track and get home again, and I tremble like a half-drowned kitten until I see a wall again, or somebody with a surly face who does not answer civilly when I speak to him. All these feelings will wear off, no doubt, and I shall be able to enter upon the new phase of my existence without any discomfort. But I was quite right to take a few months quiet retirement. One must get used to things gradually. It was the same with the champagne—to which, by the way, I had not meant to allude any further.

June 20th—It is remarkable what a fascination these very large moors have for me. It is not exactly fear any more— indeed, it must be the reverse. I do not care to be anywhere else. Instead of making this a mere pause between two different existences, I shall continue it. To that I have quite made up my mind. When I am out there in a place where I cannot see any trees, or houses, or living things, I am the last person left alive in the world. I am a kind of god. There is nobody to think at all about me, and it does not matter if my clothes are not right, or if I drop an "h"—which I rarely do except when speaking very quickly. I never knew what real independence was before. There have been too many houses around, and too many people looking on. It seems to me now such a common and despicable thing to live among people, and to have one's character and one's way altered by what they are going to think. I know now that when I ordered that bottle of champagne I did it far more to please the waiter and to make him think well of me than to please myself. I pity the kind of creature that I was then, but I had not known the open country at that time. It is a grand education. If Toller were to come in now I should say, "Go away. Go back to your bricks and mortar, and account books, and swell friends, and white waistcoats, and rubbish of that kind. You cannot possibly understand me, and your presence irritates me. If you do not go at once I will have the dog let loose upon you." By the way, that was a curious thing which happened the other day. I feed the dog, a mastiff, regularly, and it goes out with me. We had walked some way, and reached that spot where a man becomes the last man alive in the world. Suddenly the dog began to howl, and ran off home with its tail between its legs, as if it were frightened of something. What was it that the dog had seen and I had not seen? A ghost? In broad daylight? Well, if the dead come back they might walk here without contamination. A few sheep, a sweep of heather, a gray sky, but nothing that a living man planted or built. They could be alone here. If it were not that it would seem a kind of blasphemy, I would buy a piece of land in the very middle of the loneliest moor and build myself a cottage there.

June 23rd—I received a letter today from Julia. Of course she does not understand the change which has taken place in me. She writes as she always used to write, and I find it very hard to remember and realize that I liked it once, and was glad when I got a letter from her. That was before I got into the habit of going into the empty places alone. The old clerking, account book life has become too small to care about. The swell life of the private gentleman, to which I looked forward, is also not worth considering. As for Julia, I was to have married her; I used to kiss her. She wrote to say that she thought a great deal of me; she still writes. I don't want her. I don't want anything. I have become the last man alive in the world. I shall leave this farmhouse very soon. The people are all right, but they are *people*, and therefore insufferable. I can no longer live or breathe in a place where I see people, or trees which people have planted, or houses which people have built. It is an ugly word—people.

July 7th—I was wrong in saying I was the last man alive in the world. I believe I am dead. I know now why the mastiff howled and ran away. The whole moor is full of them; one sees them after a time when one has got used to the open country—or perhaps it is because one is dead. Now I see them by moonlight and sunlight, and I am not frightened at all. I think I must be dead, because there seems to be a line ruled straight through my life, and the things which happened on the further side of the line are not real. I look over this diary, and see some references to a Mr. Toller, and to some champagne, and coming into money. I cannot for the life of me think what it is all about. I suppose the incidents described really happened, unless I was mad when I wrote about them. I suppose that I am not dead, since I write in a book, and eat food, and walk, and sleep and wake again. But since I see them now—these people that fill up the lonely places—I must be quite different to ordinary human beings. If I am not dead, then what am I? Today I came across an old letter signed "Julia Jarvis"; the envelope was addressed to me. I wonder who on earth she was?

July 9th—A man in a frock coat came to see me, and talked about my best interest. He wanted me, so far as I could gather, to come away with him somewhere. He said I was all right, or, at any rate, would become all right, with a little care. He would not go away until I said I would kill him. Then the woman at the farmhouse came up with a white face, and I said I would kill her too. I positively cannot endure people. I am not alive, and I am not dead. I cannot imagine what I am.

July 16th—I have settled the whole thing to my complete satisfaction. I can without a doubt believe the evidence of my own senses. I have seen, and I have heard. I know now that I am a god. I had almost thought before that this might be. What was the matter was that I was too diffident: I had no self-confidence; I had never heard before of any man, even a clerk in an old established firm, who had become a god. I therefore supposed it was impossible until it was distinctly proved to be.

I had often made up my mind to go to that range of hills that lies to the north. They are purple when one sees them far off. At nearer view they are gray, then they become green, then one sees a silver network over the green. The silver network is made by streams descending in the sunlight. I climbed the hill slowly; the air was still, and the heat terrible.

Even the water which I drank from the running stream seemed flat and warm. As I climbed, the storm broke. I took but little notice of it, for the dead that I had met below on the moor had told me that lightning could not touch me. At the top of the hill I turned, and saw the storm raging beneath my feet. It is the greatest of mercies that I went there, for that is where the other gods gather, at such times as the lightning plays between them and the earth, and the black thunder clouds, hanging low, shut them out from the sight of men.

Some of the gods were rather like the big pictures that I have seen on the boardings advertising plays at the theater, or some food which is supposed to give great strength and muscular development. They were handsome in face, and without any expression. They never seemed to be angry or pleased, or hurt. They sat there in great long rows, resting, with the storm raging in between them and the earth. One of them was a woman. I spoke to her, and she told me that she was older than this earth; yet she had the face of a young girl, and her eyes were like eyes that I have seen before somewhere. I cannot think where I saw the eyes like those of the goddess, but perhaps it was in that part of my life which is forgotten and ruled off with a line. It gave one the greatest and most majestic feelings to stand there with the gods, and to know that one was a god one's self, and that lightning did not hurt one, and that one would live forever.

July 18th—This afternoon the storm returned, and I hurried to the meeting place, but it is far away to the hills, and though I climbed as quickly as I could the storm was almost passed, and they had gone.

August 1st—I was told in my sleep that tomorrow I was to go back to the hill again, and that once more the gods would be there, and that the storm would gather around us, and would shut us from profane sight, and the steely lightning would blind any eye that tried to look upon us. For this reason I have refused now to eat or drink anything; I am a god and have no real need of such things. It is strange that now when I see all real things so clearly and easily—the ghosts of the dead that walk across the moors in the sunlight and the concourse of the gods on the hilltop above the storm—men and women with whom I once moved before I became a god are no more to me than so many black shadows. I scarcely know one from the other, only that the presence of a black shadow anywhere near me makes me angry, and I desire to kill it. That will pass away; it is probably some faint relic of the thing that I once was in the other side of my life on the other side of the line which has been ruled across it. Seeing that I am a god it is not natural that I can feel anger or joy any more. Already all feeling of joy has gone from me, for tomorrow, so I was told in my sleep, I am to be betrothed to the beautiful goddess that is older than the world, and yet looks like a young girl, and she is to give me a sprig of heather as a token and—

It was on the evening on August 1 he was found.

"NEW YORK CITY IN THE 1930s"

An excerpt from "The Repairer of Reputations"

Robert W. Chambers

From *The King in Yellow*, 1895

Included here is an excerpt from "The Repairer of Reputations" and the complete story, "The Yellow Sign." The former selection is included for the setting, as it projects in some detail what New York City might have been in the 1930s in a parallel reality. The common thread to both stories, aside from the location, is a verse play in book form, *The King in Yellow*, which sends readers spiraling into madness and suicide, and makes manifest the lurking presence of Carcosa, just beyond our peripheral vision. Both stories are in the first person.

Toward the end of the year 1920 the Government of the United States had practically completed the program, adopted during the last months of President Winthrop's administration. The country was apparently tranquil. Everybody knows how the tariff and labor questions were settled. The war with Germany, incident on that country's seizure of the Samoan Islands, had left no visible scars upon the republic, and the temporary occupation of Norfolk by the invading army had been forgotten in the joy over repeated naval victories and the subsequent ridiculous plight of General Von Garten-laube's forces in the State of New Jersey. The Cuban and Hawaiian investments had paid one hundred percent, and the territory of Samoa was well worth its cost as a coaling station. The country was in a superb state of defense. Every coast city had been well supplied with land fortifications; the army under the parental eye of the General Staff, organized according to the Prussian system, had been increased to 300,000 men with a territorial reserve of a million; and six magnificent squadrons of cruisers and battleships patrolled the six stations of the navigable seas, leaving a steam reserve amply fitted to control home waters. The gentlemen from the West had at last been constrained to acknowledge that a college for the training of diplomats was as necessary as law schools are for the training of barristers. Consequently we were no longer represented abroad by incompetent patriots. The nation was prosperous. Chicago, for a moment paralyzed after the second great fire, had risen from its ruins, white and imperial, and more beautiful than the white city which had been built for its plaything in 1893. Everywhere good architecture was replacing bad and even in New York, a sudden craving for decency had swept away a great portion of the existing horrors. Streets had been widened, properly paved and lighted, tress had been planted, squares laid out, elevated structures demolished and underground roads built to replace them. The new government buildings and barracks were fine bits of architecture, and the long system of stone quays which completely surrounded the island had been turned into parks which proved a godsend to the population. The subsidizing of the state theater and state opera brought its own reward. The United States National Academy of Design was much like European institutions of the same kind. Nobody envied the Secretary of Fine Arts, either his cabinet position or his portfolio. The Secretary of Forestry and Game Preservation had a much easier time, thanks to the new system of National Mounted Police. We had profited well by the latest treaties with France and England; the exclusion of foreign-born Jews as a measure of national self-preservation, the settlement of the new independent Negro state of Suanee, the checking of immigration, the new laws concerning naturalization, and the gradual centralization of power in the executive all contributed to national calm and prosperity. When the Government solved the Indian problem and squadrons of Indian calvary scouts in native costume were substituted for the pitiable organizations tacked on to the tail of skeletonized regiments by a former Secretary of War, the nation drew a long sigh of relief. When, after the colossal Congress of religions, bigotry and intolerance were laid in their graves and kindness and charity began to draw warring sects together, many thought the millennium had arrived, at least in the new world, which after all is a world by itself.

But self-preservation is the first law, and the United States had to look on in helpless sorrow as Germany, Italy, Spain, and Belgium writhed in the throes of anarchy, while Russia, watching from the Caucasus, stooped and bound them one by one.

In the city of New York the summer of 1899 was signalized by the dismantling of the elevated railroads. The summer of 1900 will live in the memories of New York people for many a cycle; the Dodge Statue was removed in that year. In the following winter began that agitation for the repeal of the laws prohibiting suicide which bore its final fruit in the month of April 1920, when the first government lethal chamber was opened on Washington Square.

I had walked down that day from Dr. Archer's house on Madison Avenue, where I had been as a mere formality. Ever since that fall from my horse, four years back, I had been troubled at times with pains in the back of my head and neck, but now for months they had been absent, and the doctor sent me away that day saying there was nothing more to be cured in me. It was hardly worth his fee to be told that; I knew it myself. Still I did not grudge him the money. What I minded was the mistake which he made at first. When they picked me up from the pavement where I lay unconscious, and somebody had mercifully sent a bullet through my horse's head, I was carried to Doctor Archer, and he, pronouncing my brain affected, placed me in his private asylum where I was obliged to endure treatment for insanity. At last he decided that I was well, and I, knowing that my mind had always been as sound as his, if not sounder, "paid my tuition" as he jokingly called it, and left. I told him, smiling, that I would get even with him for his mistake, and he laughed heartily, and asked me to call once in a while. I did so, hoping for a chance to even up accounts, but he gave me none, and I told him I would wait.

The fall from my horse had fortunately left no evil results; on the contrary it had changed my whole character for the better. From a lazy young man about town, I had become active, energetic, temperate, and above all—oh, above all else—ambitious. There was only one thing which troubled me; I laughed at my own uneasiness, and yet it troubled me.

During my convalescence I had bought and read for the first time, *The King in Yellow.* I remember after finishing the first act that it occurred to me that I had better stop. I started up and flung the book into the fireplace; the volume struck the barred grate and fell open on the hearth in the firelight. If I had not caught a glimpse of the opening words in the second act I should never have finished it, but as I stooped to pick it up, my eyes became riveted to the open page, and with a cry of terror, or perhaps it was of joy so poignant that I suffered in every nerve, I snatched the thing out of the coals and crept shaking to my bedroom, where I read it and reread it, and wept and laughed and trembled with a horror which at times assails me yet. This is the thing that troubles me, for I cannot forget Carcosa where black stars hang in the heavens; where the shadows of men's thoughts lengthen in the afternoon, when the twin suns sink into the Lake of Hali; and my mind will bear forever the memory of the Pallid Mask. I pray God will curse the writer, as the writer has cursed the world with this beautiful, stupendous creation, terrible in its simplicity, irresistible in its truth—a world which now trembles before the King in Yellow. When the French government seized the translated copies which had just arrived in Paris, London, of course, became eager to read it. It is well known how the book spread like an infectious disease, from city to city, from continent to continent, barred out here, confiscated there, denounced by press and pulpit, censured even by the most advanced of literary anarchists. No definite principles had been violated in those wicked pages, no doctrine promulgated, no convictions outraged. It could not be judged by any known standard, yet, although it was acknowledged that the supreme note of art had been struck in *The King in Yellow,* all felt human nature could not bear the strain, nor thrive on words in which the essence of purest poison lurked. The very banality and innocence of the first act only allowed the blow to fall afterward with more awful effect.

It was, I remember, the thirteenth of April 1920, that the first government lethal chamber was established on the south side of Washington Square, between Wooster Street and South Fifth Avenue. The block which had formerly consisted of a lot of shabby old buildings, used as cafés and restaurants for foreigners, had been acquired by the government in the winter of 1898; the French and Italian cafés and restaurants were torn down; the whole block was enclosed by a gilded iron railing, and converted into a lovely garden with lawns, flowers, and fountains. In the center of the garden stood a small, white building, severely classical in architecture, and surrounded by thickets of flowers. Six Ionic columns supported the roof, and the single door was of bronze. A splendid marble group of "The Fates" stood before the door, the work of a young American sculptor, Boris Yvain, who had died in Paris when only twenty-three years old.

The inauguration ceremonies were in progress as I crossed University Place and entered the square. I threaded my way through the silent throng of spectators, but was stopped at Fourth Street by a cordon of police. A regiment of United States lancers were drawn up in a hollow square around the lethal chamber. On a raised tribune facing Washington Park stood the Governor of New York, and behind him were grouped the Mayor of New York and Brooklyn, the Inspector-General of Police, the Commandant of the state troops, Colonel Livingston, military aid to the President of the United States, General Blount, commanding at Governor's Island, Major-General Hamilton, commanding the garrison of New York and Brooklyn, Admiral Buffby of the fleet in the North River, Surgeon-General Lanceford, the staff of the National Free Hospital, Senators Wyse and Franklin of New York, and the Commissioner of Public Works. The tribune was surrounded by a squadron of hussars of the National Guard.

The Governor was finishing his reply to the short speech of the Surgeon-General. I heard him say: "The laws prohibiting suicide and providing punishment for any attempt at self-destruction have been repealed. The Government has seen fit to acknowledge the right of man to end an existence which may have become intolerable to him, through physical suffering or mental despair. It is believed that the community will be benefited by the removal of such people from their midst. Since the passage of this law, the number of suicides in the United States has not increased. Now that the Government has determined to establish a lethal chamber in every city, town, and village in the country, it remains to be seen whether or not that class of human creatures from whose desponding ranks new victims of self-destruction fall daily will accept the relief thus provided." He paused, and turned to the white lethal chamber. The silence in the street was absolute. "There a painless death awaits him who can no longer bear the sorrows of this life. If death is welcome let him seek it there." Then quickly turning to the military aide of the President's household, he said, "I declare the lethal chamber open," and again facing the vast crowd he cried in a clear voice: "Citizens of New York and of the United States of America, through me the Government declares the lethal chamber to be open."

The solemn hush was broken by a sharp cry of command, the squadron of hussars filed after the Governor's carriage, the lancers wheeled and formed along Fifth Avenue to wait for the commandant of the garrison, and the mounted police followed them. I left the crowd to gape and stare at the white marble death chamber, and, crossing South Fifth Avenue, walked along the western side of that thoroughfare to Bleeker Street.

THE YELLOW SIGN

Robert W. Chambers

From *The King in Yellow*, 1895

Along the shore the cloud waves break,
The twin suns sink behind the lake,
The shadows lengthen

In Carcosa.

Strange is the night where black stars rise,
And strange moons circle through the skies,
But stranger still is

Lost Carcosa.

Songs that the Hyades shall sing,
Where flap the tatters of the King,
Must die unheard in

Dim Carcosa.

Song of my soul, my voice is dead,
Die thou, unsung, as tears unshed
Shall dry and die in

Lost Carcosa.

Cassilda's son in *The King in Yellow*, Act I, Scene 2, 1895

I

Being the Contents of an Unsigned Letter Sent to the Author

There are so many things which are impossible to explain! Why should certain chords in music make me think of the brown and golden tints of autumn foliage? Why should the Mass of Sainte Cécile send my thoughts wandering among caverns whose walls blaze with ragged masses of virgin silver? What was it in the roar and turmoil of Broadway at six o'clock that flashed before my eyes the picture of a still Breton forest where the sunlight filtered through a spring foliage and Silvia bent, half curiously, half tenderly, over a small green lizard, murmuring: "To think that this also is a little ward of God!"

When I first saw the watchman his back was toward me. I looked at him indifferently until he went into the church. I paid no more attention to him than I had to any other man who lounged through Washington Square that morning, and when I shut my window and turned back to my studio I had forgotten him. Late in the afternoon, the day being warm, I raised the window again and leaned out to get a sniff of air. A man was standing in the courtyard of the church, and I noticed him again with as little interest as I had that morning. I looked across the square to where the fountain was playing and then, with my mind filled with vague impressions of trees, asphalt drives, and the moving groups of nursemaids and holiday-makers, I started to walk back to my easel. As I turned, my listless glance included the man below in the churchyard. His face was toward me now, and with a perfectly involuntary movement I bent to it. At the same moment he raised his head and looked at me. Instantly I thought of a coffin worm. Whatever it was about the man that repelled me I did not know, but the impression of a plump white grave worm was so intense and nauseating that I must have shown it in my expression, for he turned his puffy face away with a movement which made me think of a disturbed grub in a chestnut.

I went back to my easel and motioned the model to resume her pose. After working a while I was satisfied that I was spoiling what I had done as rapidly as possible, and I took a palette knife and scraped the color out again. The flesh tones were sallow and unhealthy, and I did not understand how I could have painted such sickly color into a study which before that had glowed with healthy tones.

I looked at Tessie. She had not changed, and the clear flush of health dyed her neck and cheeks as I frowned.

"Is it something I've done?" she said.

"No,—I've made a mess of this arm, and for the life of me I can't see how I came to paint such mud as that into the canvas," I replied.

"Don't I pose well?" she insisted.

"Of course, perfectly."

"Then it's not my fault?"

"No. It's my own."

"I'm very sorry," she said.

I told her she could rest while I applied rag and turpentine to the plague spot on my canvas, and she went off to smoke a cigarette and look over the illustrations in the *Courier Français*.

I did not know whether it was something in the turpentine or a defect in the canvas, but the more I scrubbed the more that gangrene seemed to spread. I worked like a beaver to get it out, and yet the disease appeared to creep from limb to limb of the study before me. Alarmed I strove to arrest it, but now the color on the breast changed and the whole figure seemed to absorb the infection as a sponge soaks up water. Vigorously I plied palette knife, turpentine, and scraper, thinking all the time what a séance I should hold with Duval who sold me the canvas which was defective nor yet the angry colors of Edward. "It must be the turpentine," I though angrily, "or else my eyes have become so blurred and confused by the afternoon light that I can't see straight." I called Tessie, the model. She came and leaned over my chair blowing rings of smoke into the air.

"What *have* you been doing to it?" she exclaimed.

"Nothing," I growled, "it must be this turpentine!"

"What a horrible color it is now," she continued. "Do you think my flesh resembles green cheese?"

"No, I don't," I said angrily, "did you ever know me to paint like that before?"

"No, indeed!"

"Well, then!"

"It must be the turpentine, or something," she admitted.

She slipped on a Japanese robe and walked to the window. I scraped and rubbed until I was tired and finally picked up my brushes and hurled them through the canvas with forcible expression, the tone alone of which reached Tessie's ears.

Nevertheless she promptly began: "That's it! Swear and act silly and ruin your brushes! You have been three weeks on that study, and now look! What's the good of ripping canvas? What creatures artists are!"

I felt about as much ashamed as I usually did after such an outbreak, and I turned the ruined canvas to the wall. Tessie helped me clean my brushes, and then danced away to dress. From the screen she regaled me with bits of advice concerning whole or partial loss of temper, until, thinking, perhaps, I had been tormented sufficiently, she came out to implore me to button her waist where she could not reach it on the shoulder.

"Everything went wrong from the time you came back from the window and talked about that horrid-looking man you saw in the churchyard," she announced.

"Yes, he probably bewitched the picture," I said, yawning. I looked at my watch.

"It's after six, I know," said Tessie, adjusting her hat before the mirror.

"Yes," I replied, "I didn't mean to keep you so long." I leaned out of the window but recoiled with disgust, for the young man with the pasty face stood below in the churchyard. Tessie saw my gesture of disapproval and leaned from the window.

"Is that the man you don't like?" she whispered.

I nodded.

"I can't see his face, but he does look fat and soft. Someway or other," she continued, turning to look at me, "he reminds me of a dream,—an awful dream I once had. Or," she mused, looking down at her shapely shoes, "was it a dream after all?"

"How should I know?" I smiled.

Tessie smiled in reply.

"You were in it," she said, "so perhaps you might know something about it."

"Tessie! Tessie!" I protested, "don't you dare flatter by saying you dream about me!"

"But I did," she insisted; "shall I tell you about it?"

"Go ahead," I replied, lighting a cigarette.

Tessie leaned back on the open window-sill and began very seriously.

"One night last winter I was lying in bed thinking about nothing at all in particular. I had been posing for you and I was tired out, yet it seemed impossible for me to sleep. I heard the bells in the city ring ten, eleven, and midnight. I must have fallen asleep about midnight because I don't remember hearing the bells after that. It seemed to me that I had scarcely closed my eyes when I dreamed that something impelled me to go to the window. I rose, and raising the sash, leaned out. Twenty-fifth Street was deserted as far as I could see. I began to be afraid; everything outside seemed so—so black and uncomfortable. Then the sound of wheels in the distance came to my ears, and it seemed to me as though that was what I must wait for. Very slowly the wheels approached, and, finally, I could make out a vehicle moving along the street. It came nearer and nearer, and when it passed beneath my window I saw it was a hearse. Then, as I trembled with fear, the driver turned and looked straight at me. When I awoke I was standing by the open window shivering with cold, but the black-plumed hearse and the driver were gone. I dreamed this dream again in March last, and again awoke beside the open window. Last night the dream came again. You remember how it was raining; when I awoke, standing at the open window, my nightdress was soaked."

"But where did I come into the dream?" I asked.

"You—you were in the coffin; but you were not dead."

"In the coffin?"

"Yes."

"How did you know? Could you see me?"

"No; I only knew you were there."

"Had you been eating Welsh rarebits, or lobster salad?" I began laughing, but the girl interrupted me with a frightened cry.

"Hello! What's up?" I said, as she shrank into the embrasure by the window.

"The—the man below in the churchyard;—he drove the hearse."

"Nonsense," I said, but Tessie's eyes were wide with terror. I went to the window and looked out. The man was gone. "Come, Tessie," I urged, "don't be foolish. You have posed too long; you are nervous."

"Do you think I could ever forget that face?" she murmured. "Three times I saw the hearse pass below my window, and every time the driver turned and looked up at me. Oh, his face was so white and—and soft? It looked dead—it looked as if it had been dead a long time."

I induced the girl to sit down and swallow a glass of Marsala. Then I sat down beside her, and tried to give her some advice.

"Look here, Tessie, " I said, "you go to the country for a week or two, and you'll have no more dreams about hearses. You pose all day, and when night comes your nerves are upset. You can't keep this up. Then again, instead of going to bed when your day's work is done, you run off to picnics at Sulzer's Park, or go to the Eldorado or Coney Island, and when you come down here next morning you are fagged out. There was no real hearse. That was a soft-shell crab dream."

She smiled faintly.

"What about the man in the churchyard?"

"Oh, he's only an ordinary unhealthy, everyday creature."

"As true as my name is Tessie Reardon, I swear to you,

Mr. Scott, that the face of the man below in the churchyard is the face of the man who drove the hearse!"

"What of it," I said. "It's an honest trade."

"Then you think I *did* see the hearse?"

"Oh," I said, diplomatically, "if you really did, it might not be unlikely that the man below drove it. There is nothing in that."

Tessie rose, unrolled her scented handkerchief, and taking a bit of gum from a knot in the hem, placed it in her mouth. Then drawing on her gloves she offered me her hand, with a frank, "Good night, Mr. Scott," and walked out.

II

The next morning, Thomas, the bellboy, brought me the *Herald* and a bit of news. The church next door had been sold. I thanked heaven for it, not that being a Catholic I had any repugnance for the congregation next door, but because my nerves were shattered by a blatant exhorter, whose very word echoed through the aisle of the church as if it had been my own rooms, and who insisted on his r's with a nasal persistence which revolted my every instinct. Then, too, there was a fiend in human shape, an organist, who reeled off some of the grand old hymns with an interpretation of his own, and I longed for the blood of a creature who could play the doxology with an amendment of minor chords which one hears only in a quartet of very young undergraduates. I believe the minister was a good man, but when he bellowed: "And the Lorrrrd said unto Moses, the Lorrrd is a man of war; the Lorrrd is his name. My wrath shall wax hot and I will kill you with the sworrrdd!" I wondered how many centuries of purgatory it would take to atone for such a sin.

"Who bought the property?" I asked Thomas.

"Nobody that I knows, sir. They do say the gent wot owns this 'ere 'Amilton flats was lookin' at it. 'E might be a bildin' more studios."

I walked to the window. The young man with the unhealthy face stood by the churchyard gate, and at the mere sight of him the same overwhelming repugnance took possession of me.

"By the way, Thomas," I said, "who is that fellow down there?"

Thomas sniffed. "That there worm, sir? 'E's night-watchman of the church, sir. 'E maikes me tired a-sittin' out all night on them steps and lookin' at you insultin' like. I'd a punched 'is 'ed, sir—beg pardon, sir—"

"Go on, Thomas."

"One night a comin' 'ome with 'Arry, the other English boy, I sees 'im a sittin' there on them steps. We 'ad Molly and Jen with us, sir, the two girls on the tray service, an' 'e looks so insultin' at us that I up and sez: 'Wat you lookin' hat, you fat slug'—beg pardon, sir, but that's 'ow I sez, sir. Then 'e don't say nothin' and I sez: 'Come out and I'll punch that puddin' 'ed.' Then I hopens the gate an' goes in, but 'e don't say nothin', only looks insultin' like. Then I 'its 'im one, but, ugh! 'is 'ed was that cold and mushy it ud sicken you to touch 'im."

"What did he do then?" I asked curiously.

"'Im? Nawthin'."

"And you, Thomas?"

The young fellow flushed with embarrassment and smiled uneasily.

"Mr. Scott, sir, I ain't no coward an' I can't make it out at all why I run. I was in the 5th Lawncers, sir, bugler at Tel-el-Kebir, an' was shot by the wells."

"You don't mean to say you ran away?"

"Yes, sir; I run."

"Why?"

"That's just what I want to know, sir. I grabbed Molly an' run, an' the rest was as frightened as I."

"But what were they frightened at?"

Thomas refused to answer for a while, but now my curiosity was aroused about the repulsive young man below and I pressed him. Three years' sojourn in America had not only modified Thomas' cockney dialect but had given him the Americans' fear of ridicule.

"You won't believe me, Mr. Scott, sir?"

"Yes, I will."

"You will lawf at me, sir?"

"Nonsense!"

He hesitated. "Well, sir, it's God's truth that when I 'it 'im 'e grabbed me wrists, sir, and when I twisted 'is soft, mushy fist one of 'is fingers come off in me 'and."

The utter loathing and horror of Thomas' face must have been reflected in my own for he added:

"It's orful, an' now when I see 'im I just go away. 'E maikes me hill."

When Thomas had gone I went to the window. The man stood beside the church railing with both hands on the gate, but I hastily retreated to my easel again, sickened and horrified, for I saw that the middle finger of his right hand was missing.

At nine o'clock Tessie appeared and vanished behind the screen with a merry "Good morning, Mr. Scott." When she reappeared and taken her pose upon the model stand I started a new canvas much to her delight. She remained silent as long as I was on the drawing, but as soon as the scrape of the charcoal ceased and I took up my fixative she began to chatter.

"Oh, I had such a lovely time last night. We went to Tony Pastor's."

"Who are 'we'?" I demanded.

"Oh, Maggie, you know, Mr. Whyte's model, and Pinkie McCormick—we call her Pinkie because she's got that beautiful red hair you artists like so much—and Lizzie Burke."

I sent a shower of spray from the fixative over the canvas, and said: "Well, go on."

"We saw Kelly and Baby Barnes the skirt dancer and—and all the rest. I made a mash."

"Then have you gone back on me, Tessie?"

She laughed and shook her head.

"He's Lizzie Burke's brother, Ed. He's a perfect gen'l'man."

I felt constrained to give her some parental advice concerning mashing, which she took with a bright smile.

"Oh, I can take care of a strange mash," she said, examining her chewing gum, "but Ed is different. Lizzie is my best friend."

Then she related how Ed had come back from the stocking mill in Lowell, Massachusetts, to find her and Lizzie grown up, and what an accomplished young man he was, and how he thought nothing of squandering half a dollar for ice cream and oysters to celebrate his entry as clerk into the woolen department of Macy's. Before she finished I began to paint, and she resumed the pose, smiling and chattering like a sparrow. By noon I had the study fairly well rubbed in and Tessie came to look at it.

"That's better," she said.

I thought so too, and ate my lunch with a satisfied feeling that all was going well. Tessie spread her lunch on a drawing table opposite me and we drank our claret from the same bottle and lighted our cigarettes from the same match. I was very much attached to Tessie. I had watched her shoot up into a slender but exquisitely formed woman from a frail, awkward child. She had posed for me during the last three years, and among all my models she was my favorite. It would have troubled me very much indeed had she become "tough" or "fly," as the phrase goes, but I never noticed any deterioration of her manner, and felt at heart that she was all right. She and I never discussed morals at all, and I had no intention of doing so, partly because I had none myself, and partly because I knew she would do what she liked to spite me. Still I did hope she would steer clear of complications, because I wished her well, and then also I had a selfish desire to retain the best model I had. I knew that mashing, as she termed it, had no significance with girls like Tessie, and that such things in America did not resemble in the least the same things in Paris. Yet, having lived with my eyes open, I also knew that somebody would take Tessie away some day, in one manner or another, and though I professed to myself that marriage was nonsense, I sincerely hoped that, in this case, there would be a priest at the end of the vista. I am a Catholic. When I listen to high mass, when I sign myself, I feel that everything, including myself, is more cheerful, and when I confess, it does me good. A man who lives as much alone as I do, must confess to somebody. Then, again, Sylvia was Catholic, and it was reason enough for me. But I was speaking of Tessie, which is very different. Tessie also was Catholic and much more devout than I, so, taking it all in all, I had little fear for my pretty model until she should fall in love. But *then* I knew that fate alone would decide her future for her, and I prayed inwardly that fate would keep her away from men like me and throw into her path nothing but Ed Burkes and Jimmy McCormicks, bless her sweet face!

Tessie sat blowing rings of smoke up to the ceiling and tinkling the ice in her tumbler.

"Do you know, Kid, that I also had a dream last night?" I observed. I sometimes called her "the Kid."

"Not about that man," she laughed.

"Exactly. A dream similar to yours, only much worse."

It was foolish and thoughtless of me to say this, but you know how little tact the average painter has.

"I must have fallen asleep about ten o'clock," I continued, "and after awhile I dreamt that I awoke. So plainly did I hear the midnight bells, the wind in the tree branches, and the whistle of steamers from the bay, that even now I can scarcely believe I was not awake. I seemed to be lying in a box which had a glass cover. Dimly I saw the street lamps as I passed, for I must tell you, Tessie, the box in which I reclined appeared to lie in a cushioned wagon which jolted me over a stony pavement. After a while I became impatient and tried to move but the box was too narrow. My hands were crossed on my breast so I could not raise them to help myself. I listened and then tried to call. My voice was gone. I could hear the trample of the horse attached to the wagon and even the breathing of the driver. Then another sound broke upon my ears like the raising of a window sash. I managed to turn my head a little, and found I could look, not only through the glass cover of my box, but also through the glass panes in the side of the covered vehicle. I saw houses, empty and silent, with neither light nor life about any of them excepting one. In that house a window was open on the first floor and a figure all in white stood looking down into the street. It was you."

Tessie had turned her face away from me and leaned on the table with her elbow.

"I could see your face," I resumed, "and it seemed to me to be very sorrowful. Then we passed on and turned into a narrow black lane. Presently the horses stopped. I waited and waited, closing my eyes with fear and impatience, but all was silent as the grave. After what seemed to me hours, I began to feel uncomfortable. A sense that somebody was close to me made me unclose my eyes. Then I saw the white face of the hearse driver looking at me through the coffin lid—"

A sob from Tessie interrupted me. She was trembling like a leaf. I saw I had made an ass of myself and attempted to repair the damage.

"Why, Tess," I said, "I only told you this to show you what influence your story might have on another person's dreams. You don't suppose I really lay in a coffin, do you? What are you trembling for? Don't you see that your dream and my unreasonable dislike for that inoffensive watchman of the church simply set my brain working as soon as I fell asleep?"

She laid her head between her arms and sobbed as if her heart would break. What a precious triple donkey I had made of myself! But I was about to break my record. I went over and put my arm about her.

"Tessie dear, forgive me," I said; "I had no business to frighten you with such nonsense. You are too sensible a girl, too good a Catholic to believe in such dreams."

Her hand tightened on mine and her head fell back upon my shoulder, but she still trembled and I petted her and comforted her.

"Come, Tess, open your eyes and smile."

Her eyes opened with a slow languid movement and met mine, but their expression was so queer that I hastened to reassure her again.

"It's all humbug, Tessie, you surely are not afraid that any harm will come to you because of that."

"No," she said, but her scarlet lips quivered.

"Then what's the matter? Are you afraid?"

"Yes. Not for myself."

"For me, then?" I demanded gaily.

"For you," she murmured in a voice almost inaudible. "I—I care for you."

At first I started to laugh, but when I understood her, a shock passed through me and I sat like one turned to stone. This was the crowning bit of idiocy I had committed. During the moment which elapsed between her reply and my answer I thought of a thousand responses to that innocent confession. I could pass it by with a laugh, I could misunderstand her and reassure her as to my health, I could simply point out that it was impossible she could love me. But my reply was quicker than my thoughts, and I might think and think now when it was too late, for I had kissed her on the mouth.

That evening I took my usual walk in Washington Park, pondering over the occurrences of the day. I was thoroughly committed. There was no back out now, and I stared the future straight in the face. I was not good, not even scrupulous, but I had no idea of deceiving either myself or Tessie. The one passion of life lay buried in the sunlit forests of Brittany. Was it buried forever? Hope cried "No!" For three years I had waited for a footstep on my threshold. Had Sylvia forgotten? "No!" cried Hope.

I said that I was not good. That is true, but still I was not exactly a comic opera villain. I had led an easygoing reckless life, taking what invited me of pleasure, deploring and sometimes bitterly regretting consequences. In one thing alone, except in my painting, was I serious, and that something which lay hidden if not lost in the Breton forests.

It was too late now for me to regret what had occurred during the day. Whatever it had been, pity, a sudden tenderness for sorrow, or the more brutal instinct of gratified vanity, it was all the same now, and unless I wished to bruise an innocent heart my path lay marked before me. The fire and strength, the depth of passion of a love which I had never even suspected, with all my imagined experience in the world, left me no alternative but to respond or send her away. Whether because I am so cowardly about giving pain to others, or whether it was that I have little of the gloomy Puritan in me, I do not know, but I shrank from disclaiming responsibility for that thoughtless kiss, and in fact had no time to do so before the gates of her heart opened and the flood poured forth. Others who habitually do their duty and find a sullen satisfaction in making themselves and everybody else unhappy, might have withstood it. I did not. I dared not. After the storm had abated I did tell her that she might better have loved Ed Burke and worn a plain gold ring, but she would not hear of it, and I thought perhaps that as long as she had decided to love somebody she could not marry, it had better be me. I, at least, could treat her with an intelligent affection, and whenever she became tired of her infatuation she could go none the worse for it. For I was decided on that point although I knew how hard it would be. I remembered the usual termination of Platonic liaisons and thought how disgusted I had been whenever I heard of one. I knew I was undertaking a great deal for so unscrupulous a man as I was, and I dreaded the future, but never for one moment did I doubt that she was safe with me. Had it been anybody but Tessie I should not have bothered my head about scruples. For it did not occur to me to sacrifice Tessie as I would have sacrificed a woman of the world. I looked the future squarely in the face and saw the several probable endings of the affair. She would either tire of the whole thing, or become so unhappy that I should have either to marry her or go away. If I married her we would be unhappy. I with a wife unsuited to me, and she with a husband unsuitable for any woman. For my past life could scarcely entitle me to marry. If I went away she might either fall ill, recover, and marry some Eddie Burke, or she might recklessly or deliberately go and do something foolish. On the other hand if she tired of me, then her whole life would be before her with beautiful vistas of Eddie Burkes and marriage rings and twins and Harlem flats and heaven knows what. As I strolled along through the trees by the Washington Arch, I decided that she should find a substantial friend in me anyway and the future could take care of itself. Then I went into the house and put on my evening dress for the faintly perfumed note on my dresser said, "Have a cab at the stage door at eleven," and the note was signed "Edith Carmichel, Metropolitan Theater, June 19th, 189—."

I took supper that night, or rather we took supper, Miss Carmichel and I, at Solari's and the dawn was just beginning to gild the cross on the Memorial Church as I entered Washington Square after leaving Edith at the Brunswick. There was not a soul in the park as I passed among the trees and took the walk which leads from the Garibaldi statue to the Hamilton Apartment House, but as I passed the churchyard

I saw a figure sitting on the stone steps. In spite of myself a chill crept over me at the sight of the white puffy face, and I hastened to pass. Then he said something which might have been addressed to me or might merely have been a mutter to himself, but a sudden furious anger flamed up within me that such a creature should address me. For an instant I felt like wheeling about and smashing my stick over his head, but I walked on, and entering the Hamilton went to my apartment. For some time I tossed about the bed trying to get the sound of his voice out of my ears, but could not. It filled my head, that muttering sound, like thick oily smoke from a fat rendering vat or an odor of noisome decay. And as I lay and tossed about, the voice in my ears seemed more distinct, and I began to understand the words he had muttered. They came to me slowly as if I had forgotten them, and at last I could make some sense out of the sounds. It was this:

"Have you found the Yellow Sign?"
"Have you found the Yellow Sign?"
"Have you found the Yellow Sign?"

I was furious. What did he mean by that? Then with a curse upon him and his I rolled over and went to sleep, but when I awoke later I looked pale and haggard, for I had dreamed the dream of the night before and it troubled me more than I cared to think.

I dressed and went down to my studio. Tessie sat by the window, but as I came in she rose and put both arms around my neck for an innocent kiss. She looked so sweet and dainty that I kissed her again and then sat down before the easel.

"Hello! Where's the study I began yesterday?" I asked.

Tessie looked conscious, but did not answer. I began to hunt among the piles of canvases, saying, "Hurry up, Tess, and get ready; we must take advantage of the morning light."

When at last I gave up the search among the other canvases and turned to look around the room for the missing study I noticed Tessie standing by the screen with her clothes still on.

"What's the matter," I asked, "don't you feel well?"

"Yes."

"Then hurry."

Then I understood. Here was a new complication. I had lost, of course, the best nude model I had ever seen. I looked at Tessie. Her face was scarlet. Alas! Alas! We had eaten of the tree of knowledge, and Eden and native innocence were dreams of the past—I mean for her.

I suppose she noticed the disappointment on my face, for she said: "I will pose if you wish. The study is behind the screen here where I put it."

"No," I said, "we will begin something now;" and I went into my wardrobe and picked out a Moorish costume which fairly blazed with tinsel. It was genuine costume, and Tessie retired to the screen with it enchanted. When she came forth again I was astonished. Her long black hair was bound above her forehead with a circlet of turquoises, and the ends curled about her glittering girdle. Her feet were encased in the embroidered pointed slippers and the skirt of her costume, curiously wrought with arabesques in silver, fell to her ankles. The deep metallic blue vest embroidered with silver and the short Mauresque jacket spangled and sewn with turquoises became her wonderfully. She came up to me and held up her face smiling. I slipped my hand into my pocket and drawing out a gold chain with a cross attached, dropped it over her head.

"It's yours, Tessie."

"Mine?" she faltered.

"Yours. Now go and pose." Then with a radiant smile she ran behind the screen and presently reappeared with a little box on which was written my name.

"I had intended to give it to you when I went home tonight," she said, "but I can't wait now."

I opened the box. On the pink cotton inside lay a clasp of black onyx, on which was inlaid a curious symbol or letter in gold. It was neither Arabic nor Chinese, nor as I found afterward did it belong to any human script.

"It's all I had to give you for a keepsake," she said, timidly.

I was annoyed, but I told her how much I should prize it, and promised to wear it always. She fastened it on my coat beneath the lapel.

"How foolish, Tess, to go and buy me such a beautiful thing as this," I said.

"I did not buy it," she laughed.

"Where did you get it?"

Then she told me how she had found it one day while coming from the aquarium in the Battery, how she had advertised it and watched the papers, but at last gave up all hopes of finding the owner.

"That was last winter," she said, "the very day I had the first horrid dream about the hearse."

I remembered my dream of the previous night but said nothing, and presently my charcoal was flying over a new canvas, and Tessie stood motionless on the model stand.

III

The following day was a disastrous one for me. While moving a framed canvas from one easel to another my foot slipped on the polished floor and I fell heavily on both wrists. They were so badly sprained that it was useless to attempt to hold a brush, and I was obliged to wander about the studio, glaring at unfinished drawings and sketches until despair seized me and I sat down to smoke and twiddle my thumbs with rage. The rain blew against the windows and rattled on the roof of the church, driving me into a nervous fit with its interminable patter. Tessie sat sewing by the window, and every now and then raised her head and looked at me with such innocent compassion that I began to feel ashamed of my irritation and looked about for something to occupy. I had read all the papers and all the books in the library, but for the sake of something to do I went to the bookcases and shoved them open with my elbow. I knew every volume by its color and examined them all, passing slowly around the library and whistling to keep up my spirits. I was turning to go into the dining room when my eye fell upon a book bound in yellow, standing in the corner of the top shelf of the last bookcase. I did not remember it and from the floor could not decipher the pale lettering on the back, so I went to the smoking room and called Tessie. She came in from the studio and climbed up to reach the book.

"What is it?" I asked.

"The King in Yellow."

I was dumbfounded. Who had placed it there? How came it into my rooms? I had long ago decided that I should never open that book, and nothing on Earth could have persuaded me to buy it. Fearful lest curiosity might tempt me to open it, I never even looked at it in bookstores. If I ever had had any curiosity to read it, the awful tragedy of young Castaigne, whom I knew, prevented me from exploring its wicked pages. I had always refused to listen to any description of it, and indeed, nobody ever ventured to discuss the second part aloud, so I had absolutely no knowledge of what those leaves might reveal. I stared at the poisonous yellow binding as I would a snake.

"Don't touch it, Tessie," I said; "come down."

Of course my admonition was enough to arouse her curiosity, and before I could prevent it she took the book and, laughing, danced away into the studio with it. I called to her but she slipped away with a tormenting smile at my helpless hands, and I followed her with some impatience.

"Tessie!" I cried, entering the library, "listen, I am serious. Put that book away. I do not wish you to open it!" The library was empty. I went into both drawing rooms, then into the bedrooms, laundry, kitchen, and finally returned to the library and began a systematic search. She had hidden herself so well that it was half an hour later when I discovered her crouching white and silent by the latticed window in the store room above. At first glance I saw she had been punished for her foolishness. *The King in Yellow* lay at her feet, but the book was open at the second part. I looked at Tessie and saw it was too late. She opened *The King in Yellow*. Then I took her by the hand and led her into the studio. She seemed dazed, and when I told her to lie down on the sofa she obeyed me without a word. After a while she closed her eyes and her breathing became regular and deep, but I could not determine whether or not she slept. For a long while I sat silently beside her, but she neither stirred nor spoke, and at last I rose and entering the unused store room took the yellow book in my least injured hand. It seemed heavy as lead, but I carried it into the studio again, and sitting down on the rug beside the sofa, opened it and read it through from the beginning to end.

When, faint with the excess of my emotions, I dropped the volume and leaned wearily back against the sofa, Tessie opened her eyes and looked at me.

We had been speaking for some time in a dull monotonous strain before I realized that we were discussing *The King in Yellow*. Oh the sin of writing such words,—words which are clear as crystal, limpid and musical as bubbling springs, words which sparkle and glow like the poisoned diamonds of the Medicis! Oh the wickedness, the hopeless damnation of a soul who could fascinate and paralyze human creatures with such words,—words understood by the ignorant and wise alike, words which are more precious than jewels, more soothing than heavenly music, more awful than death itself.

We talked on, unmindful of the gathering shadows, and she was begging me to throw away the clasp of black onyx quaintly inlaid with what we now knew to be the Yellow Sign. I never shall know why I refused, though even at this hour, her in my bedroom as I write this confession, I should be glad to know *what* it was that prevented me from tearing the Yellow Sign from my breast and casting it into the fire. I am sure I wished to do so, but Tessie pleaded with me in vain. Night fell and the hours dragged on, but still we murmured to each other of the King and the Pallid Mask, and midnight sounded from the misty spires in the fog-wrapped city. We spoke of Hastur and of Cassilda, while outside the fog rolled against the blank windowpanes as the cloud waves roll and break on the shores of Hali.

The house was very silent now and not a sound from the misty streets broke the silence. Tessie lay among the cushions, her face a gray blot in the gloom, but her hands were clasped in mine and I knew that she knew and read my thoughts as I read hers, for we had understood the mystery of the Hyades and the Phantom of Truth was laid. Then as we answered each other, swiftly, silently, thought on thought, the shadows stirred in the gloom about us, and far in the distant streets we heard a sound. Nearer and nearer it came, the dull crunching of wheels, nearer and yet nearer, and now, outside before the door it ceased, and I dragged myself to the window and saw a black plumed hearse. The gate below opened and shut, and I crept shaking to my door and bolted it, but I knew no bolts, no locks, could keep that creature out who was coming for the Yellow Sign. And now I heard him moving very softly along the hall. Now he was at the door, and the bolts rotted at his touch. Now he had entered. With eyes starting from my head I peered into the darkness, but when he came into the room I did not see him. It was only when I felt him envelop me in his cold soft grasp that I cried out and struggled with deadly fury, but my hands were useless and he tore the onyx clasp from my coat and struck me full in the face. Then, as I fell, I heard Tessie's soft cry and her spirit fled to God, and even while falling I longed to follow her, for I knew that the King in Yellow had opened his tattered mantle and there was only Christ to cry to now.

I could tell more, but I cannot see what help it will be to the world. As for me I am past human help or hope. As I lie here, writing, careless even whether or not I die before I finish, I can see the doctor gathering up his powders and vials with a vague gesture to the good priest beside me, which I understand.

They will be very curious to know the tragedy—they of the outside world who write books and print millions of newspapers, but I shall write no more, and the father confessor will seal my last words with the seal of sanctity when his holy office is done. They of the outside world may send their creatures into wrecked homes and death-smitten firesides, and their newspapers will batten on blood and tears, but with me their spies must halt before the confessional. They know that Tessie is dead and that I am dying. They know how the people in the house, aroused by an infernal scream, rushed into my room and found one living and two dead, but they do not know what I shall tell them now; they do not know that the doctor said as he pointed to a horrible decomposed heap on the floor—the livid corpse of the watchman from the church: "I have no theory, no explanation. That man must have been dead for months!"

I think I am dying. I wish the priest would—

AN INHABITANT OF CARCOSA

Ambrose Bierce

From *Can Such Things Be?*, 1909

Carcosa. It's in another world, somewhere just past our immediate perception. But in myriad ways we receive stories, images, poetry, and even artifacts from it. It has been the inspiration for dozens of writers, including most notably, Robert W. Chambers. Did Ambrose Bierce invent it? Perhaps that's where he went in 1913, when he disappeared. There are glancing references to Hali, Hastur, and other Carcosan names in other Bierce stories, suggesting that it was a world he visited with some frequency. In this instance, the first person element is introduced by means of a medium.

For there be divers sorts of death—some wherein the body remaineth; and in some it vanisheth quite away with the spirit. This commonly occurreth only in solitude (such is God's will) and, none seeing the end, we say the man is lost, or gone on a long journey—which indeed he hath; but sometimes it hath happened in the sight of many, as abundant testimony showeth. In one kind of death the spirit also dieth, and this it hath been known to do while yet the body was in vigor for many years. Sometimes, as is veritably attested, it dieth with the body, but after a season is raised up again in that place where the body did decay.

Pondering these words of Hali (whom God rest) and questioning their full meaning, as one who, having an intimation, yet doubts if there be not something behind, other than that which he has discerned, I noted not whither I had strayed until a sudden chill wind striking my face revived in me a sense of my surroundings. I observed with astonishment that everything seemed unfamiliar. On every side of me stretched a bleak and desolate expanse of plain, covered with a tall overgrowth of sere grass, which rustled and whistled in the autumn wind with heaven knows what mysterious and disquieting suggestion. Protruded at long intervals above it, stood strangely shaped and somber-colored rocks, which seemed to have an understanding with one another and to exchange looks of uncomfortable significance, as if they had reared their heads to watch the issue of some foreseen event. A few blasted trees here and there appeared as leaders in this malevolent conspiracy of silent expectation.

The day, I thought, must be far advanced, though the sun was invisible; and although sensible that the air was raw and chill my consciousness of that fact was rather mental than physical—I had no feeling of discomfort. Over all the dismal landscape a canopy of low, lead-colored clouds hung like a visible curse. In all this there were a menace and a portent—a hint of evil, an intimation of doom. Bird, beast, or insect there was none. The wind sighed in the bare branches of the dead trees and the gray grass bent to whisper its dread secret to the earth; but no other sound nor motion broke the awful repose of that dismal place.

I observed in the herbage a number of weather-worn stones, evidently shaped with tools. They were broken, covered with moss and half sunken in the earth. Some lay prostrate, some leaned at various angles, none was vertical. They were obviously headstones of graves, though the graves themselves no longer existed as either mounds or depressions; the years had leveled all. Scattered here and there, more massive blocks showed where some pompous tomb or ambitious monument had once flung its feeble defiance at oblivion. So old seemed these relics, these vestiges of vanity and memorials of affection and piety, so battered and worn and stained—so neglected, deserted, forgotten the place, that I could not help thinking myself the discoverer of the burial ground of a prehistoric race of men whose very name was long extinct.

Filled with these reflections, I was for some time heedless of the sequence of my own experiences, but I soon thought, "How came I hither?" A moment's reflection seemed to make this all clear and explain at the same time, though in a disquieting way, the singular character with which my fancy had invested all that I saw or heard. I was ill. I remembered now that I had been prostrated by a sudden fever, and that my family had told me that in my periods of delirium I had constantly cried out for liberty and air, and had been held in bed to prevent my escape out of doors. Now I had eluded the vigilance of my attendants and had wandered hither to—to where? I could not conjecture. Clearly I was at a considerable distance from the city where I dwelt—the ancient and famous city of Carcosa.

No signs of human life were anywhere visible nor audible; no rising smoke, no watchdog's bark, no lowing of cattle, no shouts of children at play—nothing but that dismal burial place, with its air of mystery and dread, due to my own disordered brain. Was I not becoming again delirious, there beyond human aid? Was it not indeed *all* an illusion of my madness? I called aloud the names of my wives and sons, reached out my hands in search of theirs, even as I walked among the crumbling stones and in the withered grass.

A noise behind me caused me to turn about. A wild animal—a lynx—was approaching. The thought came to me: If I break down here in the desert—if the fever return and I fail, this beast will be at my throat. I sprang toward it, shouting. It trotted tranquilly by within a hand's breadth of me and disappeared behind a rock.

A moment later a man's head appeared to rise out of the ground a short distance away. He was ascending the farther slope of a low hill whose crest was hardly to be distinguished from the general level. His whole figure soon came into view against the background of gray cloud. He was half naked, half clad in skins. His hair was unkempt, his beard long and ragged. In one hand he carried a bow and arrow; the other held a blazing torch with a long trail of black smoke. He walked slowly with caution, as if he feared falling into some open grave concealed by the tall grass. This strange apparition surprised but did not alarm, and taking such a course as to intercept him with the familiar salutation, "God keep you."

He gave no heed, nor did he arrest his pace.

"Good stranger," I continued, "I am ill and lost. Direct me, I beseech you, to Carcosa."

The man broke into a barbarous chant in an unknown tongue, passing on and away.

An owl on the branch of a decayed tree hooted dismally and was answered by another in the distance. Looking upward, I saw through a sudden rift in the clouds Aldebaran and Hyades! In all this there was a hint of night—the lynx, the man with the torch, the owl. Yet I saw—I saw even the stars in absence of darkness. I saw, but was apparently not seen nor heard. Under what awful spell did I exist.

I seated myself at the root of a great tree, seriously to consider what it were best to do. That I was mad I could no longer doubt, yet recognized a ground of doubt in the conviction. Of fever I had no trace. I had, withal, a sense of exhilaration and vigor altogether unknown to me—a feeling of mental and physical exaltation. My senses seemed all alert; I could feel the air as ponderous substance; I could hear the silence.

A good root of the giant tree against whose trunk I leaned as I sat held enclosed in its grasp a slab of stone, a part of which protruded into a recess formed by another root. The stone was thus partly protected from weather, though greatly decomposed. Its edges were worn round, its corner eaten away, its surface deeply furrowed and scaled. Glittering particles of mica were visible in the earth about it—vestiges of its decomposition. This stone had apparently marked the grave out of which the tree had sprung ages ago. The tree's exacting roots had robbed the grave and made the stone a prisoner.

A sudden wind pushed some dry leaves and twigs from the uppermost face of the stone; I saw the low relief letters of an inscription and bent to read it. God in heaven! *my* name in full!—the date of *my* birth!—the date of *my* death!

A level shaft of light illuminated the whole side of the tree as I sprang to my feet in terror. The sun was rising in the rosy east. I stood between the tree and his broad red disk—no shadow darkened the trunk!

A chorus of howling wolves saluted the dawn. I saw them sitting on their haunches, singly and in groups, on the summits of irregular mounds and tumult filling a half of my desert prospect and extending to the horizon. And then I knew that these were ruins of the ancient and famous city of Carcosa.

Such are the facts imparted to the medium Bayrolles by the spirit Hoseib Alar Robardin.

THE HORLA, OR MODERN GHOSTS

Guy de Maupassant

First published in 1887

"The Horla" is considered by most critics *the* classic and perhaps earliest "parallel world" tale, with its suggestion that "the reign of man is over." The title, a word de Maupassant invented, means, in French, something akin to "out there." Like most of the stories in this section, this is generally classified a horror story, but also akin to the other selections, it transcends the limited definition of the genre by taking us beyond accepted limits of imagination.

May 8. What a lovely day! I have spent all the morning lying in the grass in front of my house, under the enormous plane tree that shades the whole of it. I like this part of the country and I like to live here because I am attached to it by old associations, by those deep and delicate roots which attach a man to the soil on which his ancestors were born and died, which attach him to the ideas and usages of the place as well as to the food, to local expressions, to the peculiar twang of the peasants, to the smell of the soil, of the villages and of the atmosphere itself.

I love my house in which I grew up. From my windows I can see the Seine which flows alongside my garden, on the other side of the high road, almost through my grounds, the great and wide Seine, which goes to Rouen and Havre, and is covered with boats passing to and fro.

On the left, down yonder, lies Rouen, that large town, with its blue roofs, under its pointed Gothic towers. These are innumerable, slender or broad, dominated by the spire of the cathedral, and full of bells which sound through the blue air on fine mornings, sending their sweet and distant iron clang even as far as my home; that song of the metal, which the breeze wafts in my direction, now stronger and now weaker, according as the wind is stronger or lighter.

What a delicious morning it was!

About eleven o'clock, a long line of boats drawn by a steam tug as big as a fly, and which scarcely puffed while emitting its thick smoke, passed my gate.

After two English schooners, whose red flag fluttered in space, there came a magnificent Brazilian three-master; it was perfectly white, and wonderfully clean and shining. I saluted it, I hardly knew why, except that the sight of the vessel gave me great pleasure.

May 12. I have had a slight feverish attack for the last few days, and I feel ill, or rather I feel low-spirited.

Whence come those mysterious influences which change our happiness into discouragement, and our self confidence into diffidence? One might almost say that the air, the invisible air, is full of unknowable Powers whose mysterious presence we have to endure. I wake up in the best spirits, with an inclination to sing. Why? I go down to the edge of the water, and suddenly, after walking a short distance, I return home wretched, as if some misfortune were awaiting me there. Why? Is it a cold shiver which, passing over my skin, has upset my nerves and given me low spirits? Is it the form of the clouds, the color of the sky, or the color of the surrounding objects which is so changeable, that has troubled my thoughts as they passed before my eyes? Who can tell? Everything that surrounds us, everything that we see, without looking at it, everything that we touch, without knowing it, everything that we handle, without feeling it, all that we meet, without clearly distinguishing it, has a rapid, surprising and inexplicable effect upon us and upon our senses, and, through them, on our ideas and on our heart itself.

How profound that mystery of the Invisible is! We cannot fathom it with our miserable senses, with our eyes which are unable to perceive what is either too small or too great, too near to us, or too far from us—neither the inhabitants of a star nor of a drop of water; nor with our ears that deceive us, for they transmit to us the vibrations of the air in sonorous notes. They are fairies who work the miracle of changing these vibrations into sound, and by that metamorphosis give birth to music, which makes the silent motion of nature musical ... with our sense of smell which is less keen than that of a dog ... with our sense of taste which can scarcely distinguish the age of a wine!

Oh! If we only had other organs which would work other miracles in our favor, and what a number of fresh things we might discover around us!

May 16. I am ill, decidedly! I was so well last month! I am feverish, horribly feverish, or rather I am in a state of feverish enervation, which makes my mind suffer as much as my body. I have, continually, that horrible sensation of some impending danger, that apprehension of some coming misfortune, or of approaching death; that presentiment which is, no doubt, an attack of some illness which is still unknown, which germinates in the flesh and in the blood.

May 17. I have just come from consulting my physician, for I could no longer get any sleep. He said my pulse was rapid, my eyes dilated, my nerves highly strung, but there were no alarming symptoms. I must take a course of shower baths and of bromide of potassium.

May 25. No change! My condition is really very peculiar. As the evening comes on, an incomprehensible feeling of disquietude seizes me, just as if night concealed some threatening disaster. I dine hurriedly, and then try to read, but I do not understand the letters. Then I walk up and down my drawing room, oppressed by a feeling of confused and irresistible fear, the fear of sleep and fear of my bed.

About ten o'clock I go up to my room. As soon as I enter it I double-lock and bolt the door; I am afraid ... of what? Up to the present time I have been afraid of nothing ... I open my cupboards, and look under the bed; I listen ... to what? How strange it is that a simple feeling of discomfort, impeded or heightened circulation, perhaps the irritation of a nerve filament, a slight congestion, a small disturbance in the imperfect delicate functioning of our living machinery, may turn the most lighthearted of men into a melancholy one, and make a coward of the bravest? Then, I go to bed, and wait for sleep as a man might wait for the executioner. I wait for its coming with dread, and my heart beats and my legs tremble, while my whole body shivers beneath the warmth of the bedclothes, until all at once I fall asleep, as though one should plunge into a pool of stagnant water in order to drown. I do not feel it coming on as I did formerly, this perfidious sleep which is close to me and watching me, which is going to seize me by the head, to close my eyes and annihilate me.

I sleep—a long time—two or three hours perhaps—then a dream—no—a nightmare lays hold on me. I feel that I am in bed and asleep … I feel it and I know it … and I feel also that somebody is coming close to me, is looking at me, touching me, is getting on my bed, is kneeling on my chest, is taking my neck between his hands and squeezing it … squeezing it with all its might in order to strangle me.

I struggle, bound by that terrible sense of powerlessness which paralyzes us in our dreams; I try to cry out—but I cannot; I want to move—I cannot do so; I try, with the most violent efforts and breathing hard, to turn over and throw off this being who is crushing and suffocating me—I cannot!

And then, suddenly, I wake up, trembling and bathed in perspiration; I light a candle and find that I am alone, and after that crisis, which occurs every night, I at length fall asleep and slumber tranquilly till morning.

June 2. My condition has grown worse. What is the matter with me? The bromide does me no good, and the shower baths have no effect. Sometimes, in order to tire myself thoroughly, though I am fatigued enough already, I go for a walk in the forest of Roumare. I used to think at first that the fresh light and soft air, impregnated with the odor of herbs and leaves, would instill new blood in my veins and impart fresh energy to my heart. I turned into a broad hunting road, and then turned toward La Bouille, through a narrow path, between two rows of exceedingly tall trees, which placed a thick green, almost black, roof between the sky and me.

A sudden shiver ran through me, not a cold shiver, but a strange shiver of agony, and I hastened my steps, uneasy at being alone in the forest, afraid, stupidly and without reason, of the profound solitude. Suddenly it seemed to me as if I were being followed, that somebody was walking at my heels, close, quite close to me, near enough to touch me.

I turned around suddenly, but I was alone. I saw nothing behind me except the straight, broad path, empty and bordered by high trees, horribly empty; before me it also extended until it was lost in the distance, and looked just the same, terrible.

I closed my eyes. Why? And then I began to turn around on one heel very quickly, just like a top. I nearly fell down, and opened my eyes; the trees were dancing around me and the earth heaved; I was obliged to sit down. Then, ah! I no longer remembered how I had come! What a strange idea! What a strange, strange idea! I did not the least know. I started off to the right, and got back into the avenue which had led me into the middle of the forest.

June 3. I have had a terrible night. I shall go away for a few weeks, for no doubt a journey will set me up again.

July 2. I have come back, quite cured, and have had a most delightful trip into the bargain. I have been to Mount Saint Michel, which I had not seen before.

What a sight, when one arrives as I did, at Avranches toward the end of the day! The town stands on a hill, and I was taken into the public garden at the extremity of the town. I uttered a cry of astonishment. An extraordinary large bay lay extended before me, as far as my eyes could reach, between two hills which were lost to sight in the mist; and in the middle of this immense yellow bay, under a clear, golden sky, a peculiar hill rose up, somber and pointed in the midst of the sand. The sun had just disappeared, and under the still flaming sky appeared the outline of that fantastic rock which bears on its summit a fantastic monument.

At daybreak I went out to it. The tide was low, as it had been the night before, and I saw that wonderful abbey rise up before me as I approached it. After several hours' walking, I reached the enormous mass of rocks which supports the little town, dominated by the great church. Having climbed the steep and narrow street, I entered the most wonderful Gothic building that has ever been built to God on Earth, as large as a town, full of low rooms which seem buried beneath vaulted roofs, and lofty galleries supported by delicate columns.

I entered this gigantic granite gem, which is as light as a bit of lace, covered with towers, with slender belfries with spiral staircases, which raise their strange heads that bristle with chimeras, with devils, with fantastic animals, with monstrous flowers, to the blue sky by day, and to the black sky by night, and are connected by finely carved arches.

When I had reached the summit I said to the monk who accompanied me: "Father, how happy you must be here!" And he replied: "It is very windy here, monsieur"; and so we began to talk while watching the rising tide, which ran over the sand and covered it as with a steel cuirass.

And then the monk told me stories, all the old stories belonging to the place, legends, nothing but legends.

One of them struck me forcibly. The country people, those belonging to the Mount, declare that at night one can hear voices talking on the sands, then that one hears two goats bleating, one with a strong, the other with a weak voice. Incredulous people declare that it is nothing but the cry of the sea birds, which occasionally resembles bleatings, and occasionally, human lamentations; but belated fishermen swear that they have met an old shepherd wandering between tides on the sands around the little town. His head is completely concealed by his cloak and he is followed by a billy goat with a man's face, and a nanny goat with a woman's face, both having long, white hair and talking incessantly and quarreling in an unknown tongue. Then suddenly they cease and begin to bleat with all their might.

"Do you believe it?" I asked the monk. "I scarcely know," he replied, and I continued: "If there are other beings besides ourselves on this Earth, how comes it that we have not known it long since, or why have *you* not seen them? How is it that *I* have not seen them?" He replied: "Do we see the hundred-thousandth part of what exists? Look here; there is the wind, which is the strongest force in nature, which knocks down men, and blows down buildings, uproots trees, raises the sea into mountains of water, destroys cliffs and casts great ships on the rocks; the wind which kills, which whistles, which sighs, which roars—have you ever seen it, and can you see it? It exists for all that, however."

I was silent before this simple reasoning. That man was a philosopher, or perhaps a fool; I could not say which exactly, so I held my tongue. What he had said had often been in my own thoughts.

July 3. I have slept badly; certainly there is some feverish influence here, for my coachman is suffering in the same way as I am. When I went back home yesterday, I noticed his singular paleness, and I asked him: "What is the matter with you, Jean?" "The matter is that I never get any rest, and my nights devour my days. Since your departure, monsieur, there has been a spell over me."

However, the other servants are all well, but I am very much afraid of having another attack myself.

July 4. I am decidedly ill again; for my old nightmares have returned. Last night I felt somebody leaning on me and sucking my life from between my lips. Yes, he was sucking it out of my throat, like a leech. Then he got up, satiated, and I woke up, so exhausted, crushed and weak that I could not move. If this continues for a few days, I shall certainly go away again.

July 5. Have I lost my reason? What happened last night is so strange that my head wanders when I think of it!

I had locked my door, as I do now every evening, and then, being thirsty, I drank half a glass of water, and accidentally noticed that the water bottle was full up to the cut glass stopper.

Then I went to bed and fell into one of my terrible sleeps, from which I was aroused in about two hours by a still more frightful shock.

Picture to yourself a sleeping man who is being murdered and who wakes up with a knife in his lung, and whose breath rattles, who is covered with blood, and who can no longer breathe and is about to die, and does not understand—there you have it.

Having recovered my senses, I was thirsty again, so I lit a candle and went to the table on which stood my water bottle. I lifted it up and tilted it over my glass, but nothing came out. It was empty! It was completely empty! At first I could not understand it at all, and then suddenly I was seized by such a terrible feeling that I had to sit down, or rather I fell into a chair! Then I sprang up suddenly to look about me; then I sat down again, overcome by astonishment and fear, in front of the transparent glass bottle! I looked at it with fixed eyes, trying to conjecture, and my hands trembled! Somebody had drunk the water, but who? I? I without any doubt. It could surely only be I. In that case I was a somnambulist; I lived, without knowing it, that mysterious double life which makes us doubt whether there are not two beings in us, or whether a strange, unknowable and invisible being does not at such moments, when our soul is in a state of torpor, animate our captive body, which obeys this other being, as it obeys us, and more than it obeys ourselves.

Oh! Who will understand my horrible agony? Who will understand the emotion of a man who is sound in mind, wide awake, full of common sense, who looks in horror through the glass of a water bottle for a little water that disappeared while he was asleep? I remained thus until it was daylight, without venturing to go to bed again.

July 6. I am going mad. Again all the contents of my water bottle have been drunk during the night—or rather, I have drunk it!

But is it I? Is it I? Who could it be? Who? Oh! God! Am I going mad? Who will save me?

July 10. I have just been through some surprising ordeals. Decidedly I am mad! And yet!...

On July 6, before going to bed, I put some wine, milk, water, bread and strawberries on my table. Somebody drank—I drank—all the water and a little of the milk, but neither the wine, bread, nor the strawberries were touched.

On the seventh of July I renewed the same experiment, with the same results, and July 8, I left out the water and the milk, and nothing was touched.

Lastly, on July 9, I put only water and milk on my table, taking care to wrap up the bottles in white muslin and to tie down the stoppers. Then I rubbed my lips, my beard and my hands with pencil lead, and went to bed.

Irresistible sleep seized me, which was soon followed by a terrible awakening. I had not moved, and there was no mark of lead on the sheets. I rushed to the table. The muslin around the bottles remained intact; I undid the string, trembling with fear. All the water had been drunk, and so had the milk! Ah! Great God!...

I must start for Paris immediately.

July 12. Paris. I must have lost my head during the last few days. I must be the plaything of my enervated imagination, unless I am really a somnambulist, or that I have been under the power of one of those suggestions. In any case, my mental state bordered on madness, and twenty-four hours of Paris sufficed to restore my equilibrium.

Yesterday, after doing some business and paying some visits which instilled fresh and invigorating air into my soul, I wound up the evening at the *Théâtre Français.* A play by Alexandre Dumas the younger was being acted, and his active and powerful imagination completed my cure. Certainly solitude is dangerous for active minds. We require around us men who can think and talk. When we are alone for a long time, we people space with phantoms.

I returned along the boulevards to my hotel in excellent spirits. Amid the jostling of the crowds I thought, not without irony, of my terrors and surmises of the previous week, because I had believed—yes, I had believed—that an invisible being lived beneath my roof. How weak our brains are, and how quickly they are terrified and led into error by a small incomprehensible fact.

Instead of saying simply: "I do not understand because I do not know the cause," we immediately imagine terrible mysteries and supernatural powers.

July 14. Fête of the Republic. I walked through the streets, amused as a child at the firecrackers and flags. Still it is very foolish to be merry on a fixed date, by government decree. The populace is an imbecile flock of sheep, now stupidly patient, and now in ferocious revolt. Say to it: "Amuse your-self," and it amuses itself. Say to it: "Go and fight with your neighbor," and it goes and fights. Say to it: "Vote for the Emperor," and it votes for the Emperor, and then say to it: "Vote for the Republic," and it votes for the Republic.

Those who direct it are also stupid; only, instead of obeying men, they obey principles which can only be stupid, sterile, and false, for the very reason that they are considered as certain and unchangeable, in this world where one is certain of nothing, since light is an illusion and noise is an illusion.

July 16. I saw some things yesterday that troubled me very much.

I was dining at the house of my cousin, Madame Sablé, whose husband is colonel of the 76th Chasseurs at Limoges. There were two young women there, one of them who had married a medical man, Dr. Parent, who devotes much attention to nervous diseases and to the remarkable manifestations taking place at this moment under the influence of hypnotism and suggestion.

He related to us at some length the wonderful results obtained by English scientists and by the doctors of the Nancy school; and the facts which he adduced appeared to me so strange that I declared that I was altogether incredulous.

"We are," he declared, "on the point of discovering one of the most important secrets of nature; I mean to say, one of its most important secrets on this earth, for there are certainly others of a different kind of importance up in the stars, yonder. Ever since man has thought, ever since he has been able to express and write down his thoughts, he has felt himself close to a mystery which is impenetrable to his gross and imperfect senses, and he endeavors to supplement through his intellect the inefficiency of his senses. As long as that intellect remained in its elementary stage, these apparitions of invisible spirits assumed forms that were commonplace, though terrifying. Thence sprang the popular belief in the supernatural, the legends of wandering spirits, of fairies, of gnomes, ghosts, I might even say the legend of God; for our conceptions of the workman-creator, from whatever religion they may have come down to us, are certainly the most mediocre, the most stupid and the most incredible inventions that ever sprang from the terrified brain of any human beings. Nothing is truer than what Voltaire says: 'God made man in His own image, but man certainly paid him back in his own coin.'

"However, for rather more than a century men seemed to have had a presentiment of something new. Mesmer and some others have put us on an unexpected track, and, especially within the last two or three years, we have arrived at really surprising results."

My cousin, who is also very incredulous, smiled, and Dr. Parent said to her: "Would you like me to try and send you to sleep, madame?" "Yes, certainly."

She sat down in an easy chair, and he began to look at her fixedly, so as to fascinate her. I suddenly felt myself growing uncomfortable, my heart beating rapidly and a choking sensation in my throat. I saw Madame Sablé's eyes becoming heavy, her mouth twitching and her bosom heaving, and at the end of ten minutes she was asleep.

"Go behind her," the doctor said to me, and I took a seat behind her. He put a visiting card into her hands, and said to her: "This is a looking glass; what do you see in it?" And she replied: "I see my cousin." "What is he doing?" "He is twisting his mustache." "And now?" "He is taking a photograph out of his pocket." "Whose photograph is it?" "His own."

That was true, and the photograph had been given me that evening at the hotel.

"What is his attitude in this portrait?" "He is standing up with his hat in his hand."

She saw, therefore, on that card, on that piece of white pasteboard, as if she had seen it in a mirror.

The young women were frightened, and exclaimed: "That is enough! Quite, quite enough!"

But the doctor said to Madame Sablé authoritatively: "You will rise at eight o'clock tomorrow morning; then you will go and call on your cousin at his hotel and ask him to lend you five thousand francs which your husband demands of you, and which he will ask for when he sets out on his coming journey."

Then he woke her up.

On returning to my hotel, I thought over this curious séance, and I was assailed by doubts, not as to my cousin's absolute and undoubted good faith, for I had known her as well as if she were my own sister ever since she was a child, but as to a possible trick on the doctor's part. Had he not, perhaps, kept a glass hidden in his hand, which he showed to the young woman in her sleep, at the same time as he did the card? Professional conjurors do things that are just as singular.

So I went home and to bed, and this morning, at about half-past eight I was awakened by my valet, who said to me: "Madame Sablé has asked to see you immediately, monsieur." I dressed hastily and went to her.

She sat down in some agitation, with her eyes on the floor, and without raising her veil she said to me: "My dear cousin, I am going to ask a great favor of you." "What is it, cousin?" "I do not like to tell you, and yet I must. I am in absolute need of five thousand francs." "What, you?" "Yes, I, or rather my husband, who has asked me to procure them for him."

I was so thunderstruck that I stammered out my answers. I asked myself whether she had not really been making fun of me with Dr. Parent, if it was not merely a very well-acted farce which had been rehearsed beforehand. On looking at her attentively, however, all my doubts disappeared. She was trembling with grief, so painful was this step to her, and I was convinced that her throat was full of sobs.

I knew that she was very rich and I continued: "What! Has not your husband five thousand francs at his disposal? Come, think. Are you sure that he commissioned you to ask me for them?"

She hesitated for a few seconds, as if she were making a great effort to search her memory, and then replied: "Yes ... yes, I am quite sure of it." "Has he written to you?"

She hesitated again and reflected, and I guessed the torture of her thoughts. She did not know. She only knew that she was to borrow five thousand francs of me for her husband. So she told a lie. "Yes, he has written to me." "When, pray? You did not mention it to me yesterday." "I received his letter this morning." "Can you show it me?" "No; no ... no ... it contained private matters ... things too personal to ourselves.... I burned it." "So your husband runs into debt?"

She hesitated again, and then murmured: "I do not know." Thereupon I said bluntly: "I have not five thousand francs at my disposal at this moment, my dear cousin."

She uttered a kind of cry as if she were in pain and said: "Oh! oh! I beseech you, I beseech you to get them for me...."

She got excited and clasped her hands as if she were praying to me! I heard her voice change its tone; she wept and stammered, harassed and dominated by the irresistible order that she had received.

"Oh! oh! I beg you to ... if you knew what I am suffering ... I want them today."

I had pity on her: "You shall have them by and by. I swear to you." "Oh! thank you! thank you! How kind you are."

I continued: "Do you remember what took place at your house last night?" "Yes." "Do you remember that Dr. Parent sent you to sleep?" "Yes." "Oh! Very well, then; he ordered you to come to me this morning to borrow five thousand francs, and at this moment you are obeying that suggestion."

She considered for a few moments, and then replied: "But as it is my husband who wants them—"

For a whole hour I tried to convince her, but could not succeed, and when she had gone I went to the doctor. He was just going out, and he listened to me with a smile, and said: "Do you believe now?" "Yes, I cannot help it." "Let us go to your cousin's."

She was already half asleep on a reclining chair, overcome with fatigue. The doctor felt her pulse, looked at her for some time with one hand raised toward her eyes, which she closed by degrees under the irresistible power of this magnetic influence, and when she was asleep, he said:

"Your husband does not require the five thousand francs any longer! You must, therefore, forget that you asked your cousin to lend them to you, and, if he speaks to you about it, you will not understand him."

Then he woke her up, and I took out a pocketbook and said: "Here is what you asked me for this morning, my dear cousin." But she was so surprised that I did not venture to persist; nevertheless, I tried to recall the circumstance to her, but she denied it vigorously, thought I was making fun of her, and, in the end, very nearly lost her temper.

There! I have just come back, and I have not been able to eat any lunch, for this experiment has altogether upset me.

July 19. Many people to whom I told the adventure laughed at me. I no longer know what to think. The wise man says: "It may be!"

July 21. I dined at Bougival, and then I spent the evening at a boatman's ball. Decidedly everything depends on place and surroundings. It would be the height of folly to believe in the supernatural on the Ile de la Grenouillière … but on the top of Mount Saint Michel?… and in India? We are terribly influenced by our surroundings. I shall return home next week.

July 30. Nothing new; it is splendid weather, and I spend my days in watching the Seine flowing past.

August 4. Quarrels among my servants. They declare that the glasses are broken in the cupboards at night. The footman accuses the cook, who accuses the seamstress, who accuses the other two. Who is the culprit? It is a clever person who can tell.

August 6. This time I am not mad. I have seen … I have seen … I have seen!… I can doubt no longer … I have seen it!…

I was walking at two o'clock among my rose trees, in the full sunlight … in the walk bordered by autumn roses which are beginning to fall. As I stopped to look at a Géant de Bataille, which had three splendid blossoms, I distinctly saw the stalk of one of the roses near me bend, as if an invisible hand had bent it, and then break, as if that hand picked it! Then the flower raised itself, following the curve which a hand would have described in carrying it toward a mouth, and it remained suspended in the transparent air, all alone and motionless, a terrible red spot, three yards from my eyes. In desperation I rushed at it to take it! I found nothing; it had disappeared. Then I was seized with furious rage against myself, for a reasonable and serious man should not have such hallucinations.

But was it an hallucination? I turned around to look for the stalk, and I found it at once, on the bush, freshly broken, between two other roses which remained on the branch. I returned home then, my mind greatly disturbed; for I am certain now, as certain as I am of the alternation of day and night, that there exists close to me an invisible being that lives on milk and water, that can touch objects, take them and change their places; that is, consequently, endowed with a material nature, although it is imperceptible to our senses, and that lives as I do, under my roof—

August 7. I slept tranquilly. He drank my water out of the decanter, but did not disturb my sleep.

I wonder if I am mad. As I was walking just now in the sun by the riverside, doubts as to my sanity arose in me; not vague doubts such as I have had hitherto, but definite, absolute doubts. I have seen mad people, and I have known some who have been quite intelligent, lucid, even clear-sighted in every concern of life, except on one point. They spoke clearly, readily, profound on everything, when suddenly their mind struck upon the shoals of their madness and broke to pieces there, and scattered and floundered in that furious and terrible sea, full of rolling waves, fogs and squalls, which is called *madness.*

I certainly should think that I was mad, absolutely mad, if I were not conscious, did not perfectly know my condition, did not fathom it by analyzing it with the most complete lucidity. I should, in fact, be only a rational man who was laboring under an hallucination. Some unknown disturbance must have arisen in my brain, one of these disturbances which physiologists of the present day try to note and to verify; and that disturbance must have caused a deep gap in my mind and in the sequence and logic of my ideas. Similar phenomena occur in dreams which lead us among the most unlikely phantasmagoria, without causing us any surprise, because our verifying apparatus and our organ of control are asleep, while our imaginative faculty is awake and active. Is it not possible that one of the imperceptible notes of the cerebral keyboard has been paralyzed in me? Some men lose the recollection of proper names, of verbs, or of numbers, or merely of dates, in consequence of an accident. The localization of all the variations of thought has been established nowadays; why, then, should it be surprising if my faculty of controlling the unreality of certain hallucinations were dormant in me for the time being?

I thought of all this as I walked by the side of the water. The sun shone brightly on the river and made earth delightful, while it filled me with a love for life, for the swallows, whose agility always delights my eye, for the plants by the riverside, the rustle of whose leaves is a pleasure to my ears.

By degrees, however, an inexplicable feeling of discomfort seized me. It seemed as if some unknown force were numbing and stopping me, were preventing me from going further, and were calling me back. I felt that painful wish to return which oppresses you when you have left a beloved invalid at home, and when you are seized with a presentiment that he is worse.

I, therefore, returned in spite of myself, feeling certain that I should find some bad news awaiting me, a letter or a telegram. There was nothing, however, and I was more surprised and uneasy than if I had had another fantastic vision.

August 8. I spent a terrible evening yesterday. He does not show himself any more, but I feel that he is near me, watching me, looking at me, penetrating me, dominating me, and more redoubtable when he hides himself thus than if he were to manifest his constant and invisible presence by supernatural phenomena. However, I slept.

August 9. Nothing, but I am afraid.

August 10. Nothing; what will happen tomorrow?

August 11. Still nothing; I cannot stop at home with this fear hanging over me and these thoughts in my mind; I shall go away.

August 12. Ten o'clock at night. All day long I have been trying to get away, and have not been able. I wished to accomplish this simple and easy act of freedom—to go out—to get into my carriage in order to go to Rouen—and I have not been able to do it. What is the reason?

August 13. When one is attacked by certain maladies, all the springs of our physical being appear to be broken, all our energies destroyed, all our muscles relaxed; our bones, too, have become as soft as flesh, and our blood as liquid as water. I am experiencing these sensations in my moral being in a strange and distressing manner. I have no longer any strength, any courage, any self-control, not even any power to set my own will in motion. I have no power left to will anything; but some one does it for me and I obey.

August 14. I am lost! Somebody possesses my soul and dominates it. Somebody orders all my acts, all my movements, all my thoughts. I am no longer anything in myself, nothing except an enslaved and terrified spectator of all the things I do. I wish to go out; I cannot. He does not wish to, and so I remain, trembling and distracted, in the armchair in which he keeps me sitting. I merely wish to get up and to rouse myself; I cannot! I am riveted to my chair, and my chair adheres to the ground in such a manner that no power could move us.

Then, suddenly, I must, I must go to the bottom of my garden to pick some strawberries and eat them, and I go there. I pick the strawberries and eat them! Oh, my God! My God! Is there a God? If there be one, deliver me! Save me! Succor me! Pardon! Pity! Mercy! Save me! Oh, what sufferings! What torture! What horror!

August 15. This is certainly the way in which my poor cousin was possessed and controlled when she came to borrow five thousand francs of me. She was under the power of a strange will which had entered into her, like another soul, like another parasitic and dominating soul. Is the world coming to an end?

But who is he, this invisible being that rules me? This unknowable being, this rover of a supernatural race?

Invisible beings exist, then! How is it, then, that since the beginning of the world they have never manifested themselves precisely as they do to me? I have never read of anything that resembles what goes on in my house. Oh, if I could only leave it, if I could only go away, escape, and never return! I should be saved, but I cannot.

August 16. I managed to escape today for two hours, like a prisoner who finds the door of his dungeon accidentally open. I suddenly felt that I was free and that he was far away, and so I gave orders to harness the horses as quickly as possible, and I drove to Rouen. Oh, how delightful to be able to say to a man who obeys you: "Go to Rouen!"

Then, as I was getting into my carriage, I intended to say: "To the railway station!" but instead of this I shouted—I did not say, but I shouted—in such a loud voice that all the passersby turned around: "Home!" and I fell back on the cushion of my carriage, overcome by mental agony. He had found me again and regained possession of me.

August 17. Oh, what a night! What a night! And yet it seems to me that I ought to rejoice. I read until one o'clock in the morning! Herestauss, doctor of philosophy and theogony, wrote the history of the manifestation of all those invisible beings which hover around man, or of whom he dreams. He describes their origin, their domain, their power; but none of them resembles the one which haunts me. One might say that man, ever since he began to think, has had a foreboding fear of a new being, stronger than himself, his successor in this world, and that, feeling his presence, and not being able to foresee the nature of that master, he has, in his terror, created the whole race of occult beings, vague phantoms born of fear.

Having, therefore, read until one o'clock in the morning, I went and sat down at the open window, in order to cool my forehead and my thoughts, in the calm night air. It was very pleasant and warm! How I should have enjoyed such a night formerly!

There was no moon, but the stars darted out their rays in the dark heavens. Who inhabits those worlds? What forms, what living beings, what animals are there yonder? What do the thinkers in those distant worlds know more than we do? What can they do more than we can? What do they see which we do not know? Will not one of them, some day or other, traversing space, appear on our earth to conquer it, just as the Norsemen formerly crossed the sea in order to subjugate nations more feeble than themselves?

We are so weak, so defenseless, so ignorant, so small, we who live on this particle of mud which revolves in a drop of water.

I fell asleep, dreaming thus in the cool night air, and when I had slept for about three quarters of an hour, I opened my eyes without moving, awakened by I know not what confused and strange sensation. At first I saw nothing, and then suddenly it appeared to me as if a page of a book which had remained open on my table turned over of its own accord. Not a breath of air had come in at my window, and I was surprised, and waited. In about four minutes, I saw, I saw, yes, I saw with my own eyes, another page lift itself up and fall down on the others, as if a finger had turned it over. My armchair was empty, appeared empty, but I knew that he was there, he, and sitting in my place, and that he was reading. With a furious bound, the bound of an enraged wild beast that springs at its tamer, I crossed my room to seize him, to strangle him, to kill him! But before I could reach it, the chair fell over as if somebody had run away from me—my table rocked, my lamp fell and went out, and my window closed as if some thief had been surprised and fled out into the night, shutting it behind him.

So he had run away; he had been afraid; he, afraid of me!

But—but—tomorrow—or later—some day or other—I should be able to hold him in my clutches and crush him against the ground! Do not dogs occasionally bite and strangle their masters?

August 18. I have been thinking the whole day long. Oh, yes, I will obey him, follow his impulses, fulfill all his wishes, show myself humble, submissive, a coward. He is the stronger; but the hour will come—

August 19. I know—I know—I know all! I have just read the following in the *Revue du Monde Scientifique:* "A curious piece of news comes to us from Rio de Janeiro. Madness, an epidemic of madness, which may be compared to that contagious madness which attacked the people of Europe in the Middle Ages, is at this moment raging in the Province of São Paolo. The terrified inhabitants are leaving their houses, saying that they are pursued, possessed, dominated like human cattle by invisible, though tangible beings, a species of vampire, which feed on their life while they are asleep, and who, besides, drink water and milk without appearing to touch any other nourishment.

"Professor Don Pedro Henriques, accompanied by several medical savants, has gone to the Province of São Paolo, in order to study the origin and the manifestations of this surprising madness on the spot, and to propose such measures to the Emperor as may appear to him to be most fitted to restore the mad population to reason."

Ah! Ah! I remember now that fine Brazilian three-master which passed in front of my windows as it was going up the Seine, on the eighth day of last May! I thought it looked so pretty, so white and bright! That Being was on board of her, coming from there, where its race originated. And it saw me! It saw my house which was also white, and it sprang from the ship on to the land. Oh, merciful heaven!

Now I know, I can divine. The reign of man is over, and he has come. He who was feared by primitive man; evoked on dark nights, without having seen him appear, to whom the imagination of the transient masters of the world lent all the monstrous or graceful forms of gnomes, spirits, genii, fairies and familiar spirits. After the coarse conceptions of primitive fear, more clear-sighted men foresaw it more clearly. Mesmer divined it, and ten years ago physicians accurately discovered the nature of his power, even before he exercised it himself. They played with this new weapon of the Lord, the sway of a mysterious will over the human soul, which had become a slave. They called it magnetism, hypnotism, suggestion—what do I know? I have seen them amusing themselves like rash children with this horrible power! Woe to us! Woe to man! He has come, the—the—what does he call himself—the—I fancy that he is shouting out his name to me and I do not hear him—the—yes—he is shouting it out—I am listening—I cannot—he repeats it—the—Horla—I hear—the Horla—it is he—the Horla—he has come!

Ah! the vulture has eaten the pigeon; the wolf has eaten the lamb; the lion has devoured the sharp-horned buffalo; man has killed the lion with an arrow, with a sword, with gunpowder; but the Horla will make of man what we have made of the horse and of the ox; his chattel, his slave and his food, by the mere power of his will. Woe to us!

But, nevertheless, the animal sometimes revolts and kills the man who has subjugated it. I should also like—I shall be able to—but I must know him, touch him, see him! Scientists say that animals' eyes, being different from ours, do not distinguish objects as ours do. And my eye cannot distinguish this newcomer who is oppressing me.

Why? Oh, now I remember the words of the monk at Mount Saint Michel: "Can we see the hundred-thousandth part of what exists? See here; there is the wind, which is the strongest force in nature, which knocks men, and blows down buildings, uproots trees, raises the sea into mountains

of water, destroys cliffs and casts great ships on the break-
ers; the wind which kills, which whistles, which sighs, which
roars—have you ever seen it, and can you see it? It exists for
all that, however!"

And I went on thinking; my eyes are so weak, so imperfect, that they do not even distinguish hard bodies, if they
are as transparent as glass! If a glass without tinfoil behind
it were to bar my way, I should run into it, just as a bird
which has flown into a room breaks its head against the windowpanes. A thousand things, moreover, deceive man and
lead him astray. Why should it then be surprising that he
cannot perceive an unknown body through which the light
passes?

A new being! Why not? It was assuredly bound to come!
Why should we be the last? We do not distinguish it any
more than all the others created before us! The reason is, that
its nature is more perfect, its body finer and more finished
than ours, that ours is so weak, so awkwardly constructed,
encumbered with organs that are always tired, always on
the strain like machinery that is too complicated, which lives
like a plant and like a beast, nourishing itself with difficulty
on air, herbs and flesh, an animal machine which is prey to
maladies, to malformations, to decay; broken-winded, badly
regulated, simple and eccentric, ingeniously badly made, at
once a coarse and a delicate piece of workmanship, the rough
sketch of a being that might become intelligent and grand.

We are only a few, so few in this world, from the oyster up
to man. Why should there not be one more, once that period
is passed which separates the successive apparitions from
all the different species?

Why not one more? Why not, also, other trees with
immense, splendid flowers, perfuming whole regions? Why

not other elements besides fire, air, earth and water? There are four, only four, those nursing fathers of various beings! What a pity! Why are there not forty, four hundred, four thousand? How poor everything is, how mean and wretched! grudgingly produced, roughly constructed, clumsily made! Ah, the elephant and the hippopotamus, what grace! And the camel, what elegance!

But the butterfly, you will say, a flying flower! I dream of one that should be as large as a hundred worlds, with wings whose shape, beauty, colors and motion I cannot even express. But I see it—it flutters from star to star, refreshing them and perfuming them with the light and harmonious breath of its flight! And the people up there look at it as it passes in an ecstasy of delight!

What is the matter with me? It is he, the Horla, who haunts me, and who makes me think of these foolish things! He is within me, he is becoming my soul; I shall kill him!

August 19. I shall kill him. I have seen him! Yesterday I sat down at my table and pretended to write very assiduously. I knew quite well that he would come prowling around me, quite close to me, so close that I might perhaps be able to touch him, to seize him. And then—then I should have the strength of desperation; I should have my hands, my knees, my chest, my forehead, my teeth to strangle him, to crush him, to bite him, to tear him to pieces. And I watched for him with all my overexcited senses.

I had lighted my two lamps and the eight wax candles on my mantelpiece, as if with this light I could discover him.

My bedstead, my oak post bedstead, stood opposite to me; on my right was the fireplace; on my left, the door which was carefully closed, after I had left it open for some time in order to attract him; behind me was a very high wardrobe with a looking glass in it, before which I stood to shave and dress every day, and in which I was in the habit of glancing at myself from head to foot every time I passed it.

I pretended to be writing in order to deceive him, for he was also watching me, and suddenly I felt—I was certain that he was reading over my shoulder, that he was there, touching my ear.

I got up, my hands extended, and turned around so quickly that I almost fell. Eh! Well? It was as bright as at midday, but I did not see my reflection in the mirror! It was empty, clear, profound, full of light! But my figure was not reflected in it—and I, I was opposite to it! I saw the large, clear glass from top to bottom, and I looked at it with unsteady eyes; and I did not dare to advance; I did not venture to make a movement, feeling that he was there, but that he would escape again, he whose imperceptible body had absorbed my reflection.

How frightened I was! And then, suddenly, I began to see myself in a mist in the depths of the looking glass, in a mist as it were a sheet of water; and it seemed to me as if this water were flowing clearer every moment. It was like the end of an eclipse. Whatever it was that hid me did not appear to possess any clearly defined outlines, but a sort of opaque transparency which gradually grew clearer.

At last I was able to distinguish myself completely, as I do every day when I look at myself.

I had seen it! And horror of it remained with me, and makes me shudder, even now.

August 20. How could I kill it, as I could not get hold of it? Poison? But it would see me mix it with water; and then, would our poisons have any effect on its impalpable body? No—no—no doubt about the matter—Then—then?—

August 21. I sent for a blacksmith from Rouen, and ordered iron shutters for my room, such as some private hotels in Paris have on the ground floor, for fear of burglars, and he is going to make me an iron door as well. I have made myself out a coward, but I do not care about that!

September 10. Rouen, Hotel Continental. It is done—it is done—but is he dead? My mind is thoroughly upset by what I have seen.

Well then, yesterday, the locksmith having put on the iron shutters and door, I left everything open until midnight, although it was getting cold.

Suddenly I felt that he was there, and joy, mad joy, took possession of me. I got up softly, and walked up and down for some time, so that he might not suspect anything; then I took off my boots and put on my slippers carelessly; then I fastened the iron shutters, and, going back to the door, quickly double-locked it with a padlock, putting the key into my pocket.

Suddenly I noticed that he was moving restlessly around me, that in his turn he was frightened and was ordering me to let him out. I nearly yielded; I did not, however, but, putting my back to the door, I half opened it, just enough to allow me to go out backward, and as I am very tall my head touched the casing. I was sure that he had not been able to escape, and I shut him up quite alone, quite alone. What happiness! I had him fast. Then I ran downstairs; in the drawing room, which was under my bedroom, I took the two lamps and I poured the oil on the carpet, the furniture, everywhere; then I set fire to it and made my escape, after having carefully double-locked the door.

I went and hid myself at the bottom of the garden, in a clump of laurel bushes. How long it seemed! How long it seemed! Everything was dark, silent, motionless, not a breath of air and not a star, but heavy banks of clouds which one could not see, but which weighed, oh, so heavily on my soul.

I looked at my house and waited. How long it was! I already began to think that the fire had gone out of its own accord, or that he had extinguished it, when one of the lower windows gave way under the violence of the flames, and a long, soft, caressing sheet of red flame mounted up the white wall, and enveloped it as far as the roof. The light fell on the trees, the branches, and the leaves, and a shiver of fear pervaded them also! The birds awoke, a dog began to howl, and it seemed to me as if the day were breaking! Almost immediately two other windows flew into fragments, and I saw that the whole of the lower part of my house was nothing but a terrible furnace. But a cry, a horrible, shrill, heartrending cry, a woman's cry, sounded through the night, and two garret windows were opened! I had forgotten the servants! I saw their terror-stricken faces, and their arms waving frantically.

Then, overwhelmed with horror, I set off to run to the village, shouting: "Help! help! fire! fire!" I met some people who were already coming to the scene, and I returned with them.

By this time the house was nothing but a horrible and magnificent funeral pile, a monstrous funeral pile which lit up the whole country, a funeral pile where men were burning, and where he was burning also, He, He, my prisoner, that new Being, the new master, the Horla!

Suddenly the whole roof fell in between the walls, and a volcano of flames darted up to the sky. Through all the windows which opened on that furnace, I saw the flames darting, and I thought that he was there, in that kiln, dead.

Dead? Perhaps?— His body? Was not his body, which was transparent, indestructible by such means as would kill ours?

If he were not dead?—Perhaps time alone has power over that Invisible and Redoubtable Being. Why this transparent, unrecognizable body, this body belonging to a spirit, if it also has to fear ills, infirmities and premature destruction?

Premature destruction? All human terror springs from that! After man, the Horla. After him who can die every day, at any hour, at any moment, by any accident, came the one who would die only at his own proper hour, day, and minute, because he had touched the limits of his existence!

No—no—without any doubt—he is not dead— Then— then—I suppose I must kill myself! . . .

Stefan Rudnicki is the author of eleven published books including the bestselling *Sun Tzu's The Art of War* and *Wilde, the Novel*. He served as the editor of three collections of actors' resource materials for Penguin and co-authored (with Judith Cummings) *Colin Powell and the American Dream*, which sold over 350,000 copies. An avid fan of science fiction and fantasy since the mid-fifties, Stefan has produced hundreds of audiobooks, collaborating with such luminaries as Ben Bova, Orson Scott Card, and Ursula K. Le Guin.

Mr. Rudnicki has received many awards for his work in audio production and film and stage direction. His accomplishments have been recognized with The Bram Stoker Award, The Ray Bradbury Prize, and a Grammy for Best Spoken Word Album for Children, among others.

Harlan Ellison has written or edited more than seventy books, 1,700 stories, essays, and articles, and dozens of screenplays and teleplays. He has won more awards for imaginative literature than any other living author, including the Edgar, Hugo, Nebula, and Bram Stoker Awards.

.